JACKSON & JENKS
MASTER MAGICIANS

JACKSON & JENKS
MASTER MAGICIANS

DAN FRISCHMAN

This is a work of fiction. Any resemblance to actual
persons, living or dead, is entirely coincidental.

For further information:
J. J. Ross Books
P.O. BOX 1764
Burbank, CA 91507-1764

Publisher's Cataloging-in-Publication
(Provided by Quality Books, Inc.)

Frischman, Dan.
    Jackson & Jenks : master magicians / by Dan
Frischman. — 1st ed.
    p. cm.
SUMMARY: Darren Jackson and Jamie Jenks are inseparable
teenage friends who team up to perform as a magic duo. One
day, a mysterious force turns Jamie into a real magician. The
boys' instant fame causes more world reaching chaos than they
could possibly have imagined.
    LCCN 2007931300
    ISBN-13: 978-0-9796296-0-0
    ISBN-10: 0-9796296-0-8

    1. Teenage boys—Juvenile fiction. 2. Magicians—
Juvenile fiction. 3. Magic—Juvenile fiction.
4. Science fiction, American. [1. Teenage boys—Fiction.
2. Magicians—Fiction. 3. Magic—Fiction.] I. Title.
II. Title. Jackson and Jenks.

PZ7.F9172Jac 2009   [Fic]
                    QBI08-600310

For my mother
who taught us well

Contents

Imagination is the true magic carpet.
—Norman Vincent Peale

Disbelief in magic can force a poor soul into believing in government and business.
—Tom Robbins

CHAPTER 1

The Super Sucker

JAMIE JENKS found a weekend job at the last convenience store of its kind in Washington, D.C.—or, perhaps, the last of its kind anywhere. It sold the usual magazines, gifts, pills, and groceries, and also featured a full-service food counter with a dozen bar stools. Jamie's job description alternated, at various times of the day, between short-order cook, stock boy, soda jerk, clerk, and his least favorite, janitor.

At the moment, the thin, fresh-faced fifteen-year-old was in full chef mode, burdened with a packed-in lunch crowd. He worked swiftly, his raggedy blond hair flapping about as he sliced BLT sandwiches, poured coffee and tea, ladled out clam chowder, and slapped burgers onto the grill. Jamie always worked hard, but made sure to enjoy himself, too.

"One chili dog!" he shouted gleefully. "Pig in a blanket, can't really spank it, tried to caress it, got me arrested!"

The customers laughed as Jamie tossed a chili dog onto

the grill, cranking the volume of the sizzling fat.

"Went off to jail, sat on a nail, got up and then, sat down again!" Everyone enjoyed his antics, with the certain exception of the one man he really needed to please.

"Jamie!" snapped his curly-peppery-haired sixty-something boss, Mike, from behind the cash register at the far end of the counter.

"Yeah, boss?" said Jamie, deftly flipping a chain of cheese-burgers.

"That's enough of your poetry. Put a lid on it before you're singing out on the sidewalk." Mike slammed the register shut and went off to help a customer who was holding the dairy fridge open way too long.

"Puttin' on the lid," complied Jamie, then muttering, "Probably make more money on the sidewalk." A few customers grinned, but Jamie tried to take the warning seriously—summer vacation was rapidly approaching, and competition for jobs was fierce.

His employment track record was spotty at best. Two weeks ago, he was a bellhop at a posh hotel and was fired after only four hours for giving children high-speed joyrides on a luggage cart. Jamie aimed to please, but his sky-high energy level often resulted in mischievous, if innocent, antics and horseplay.

"Hey, Jamie, how about my soup?" said a hungry customer. "The Yankee Bean."

"Definite up and comer!" said Jamie, heading toward the stove. Despite his boss's warning, however, he couldn't stop himself from more rhyming and dancing. "Yankee Bean, the music machine, makes ya gong from here to Hong Kong!"

The customers cracked up at this one. Mike looked over and shook his head.

ON THE OTHER SIDE OF TOWN, Jamie's best friend, Darren Jackson, was having a lot less fun. He thought that becoming a waiter at Jimmy Giraffe's—"Where Kids Roam Free in the Jungle"—would be a painless way to rake in some easy cash. Taking orders from the swarms of rambunctious, hyper children who roamed free in the place, however, was proving to be neither easy nor painless. Kids ran about with little, if any, parental guidance, and didn't seem to mind when they would accidentally barrel into the waiters. Darren figured that actual jungles would be less savage places to work.

This was a far cry from where Darren, an honor student (at least when he applied himself, which was usually only when a reward of electronic gizmos was offered), had hoped to be at this point in his fifteen-year-old life. His major goal was to become a millionaire by the time he was twenty. The slightly overweight, curly-haired boy had mapped out his quest at age ten with a five-page "Mission Statement"—

The Darren Jackson Road to Riches Plan. Phase One: Sell my amazing inventions and invest the money in railroads and utilities, and buy houses and hotels. (Later phases involved buying airlines, skyscrapers, and small exotic islands.)

So far, though, with only a few dollars in the bank, his goal seemed to be going the way of his failed inventions. His attempts seemed great at the time—flying wings for skateboards, walkie-talkies that appeared to be candy bars, and soap that keeps you clean for a week with only one washing. But he had one more invention ready to go—a mechanical broom, made mostly out of junkyard scraps and discarded motors from appliance repair shops. Still, extra parts and equipment cost most of what he and Jamie had, but he was sure his new machine would make them both "insanely rich."

For the moment, however, he had to settle for waiting tables while wearing a goofy orange and white giraffe suit. The animal's plastic head towered above him; his own face protruded from a hole in the bottom of its long neck. As usual, he was sweating profusely under the thick, furry cloth. Still, he was trying his best to be patient with a birthday party group of fourteen unruly kids. (The sole adult in the group, occupied with a crying baby at the far end of the table, was not going to be any help.) He took an order from a freckle-faced boy with a red party hat and a cardboard pin on his shirt that read BIRTHDAY BIGSHOT.

"Which would you like—a Giraffe Burger or a Giraffe Dog?" Darren asked sweetly.

"I want three Giraffe Dogs!" announced the boy. "And put lots of mustard on them!"

Darren pointed to a yellow bottle on the table. "Okay, the mustard's right there, and you can put as much on them as you like."

"I want you to do it!"

"Well, I would, but I don't know how much you'll want on them," explained Darren.

"I don't care! You do it!"

"Well, I would, but see, that's not what I do. I just bring your Giraffe Dogs here, and then *you* squeeze the mustard on there yourself till you're all happy and satisfied." He plastered a wide smile across his face, masking his irritation.

"No!" barked the boy. "I want *you* to squeeze it, ya jerky giraffe!" The boy's friends offered ear-piercing laughter. Before Darren could respond, the boy stomped hard on his foot.

"Aaaaaaaaaaaaaaah!" cried Darren, prompting more laughter from the table. Another child stomped on his other foot. "Baaaheyyyyyy!" Darren yelled, much to the children's amusement. "All right, that's it!" he erupted. "Maybe you can all just go into the kitchen and order the food yourselves, huh? How would you like *that?*"

"What's going on here, Darren?" uttered a voice behind him.

Darren swung around and found himself face-to-face with a slim twenty-one-year-old boy with a nametag that read *Calvert—Assistant Manager.* Calvert was very prim and proper in a blue short sleeve business shirt and plain navy slacks.

"Oh, nothing, uh, Calvert. This young guest stepped on my foot, and then this one here—"

"No, I didn't!" spouted the boy. "I didn't do anything!" His friends concurred, declaring Darren a liar.

"What?" protested Darren. "I was trying to take his order and he just—"

"Oh, you tried to take his order, huh?" snipped Calvert, folding his arms. "Is that why they all have to go to the kitchen themselves? I think you owe these children an apology, Darren."

The kids gleefully chimed in. "Yeah, you do! Apologize, giraffe!"

Darren was trapped. "I'm . . . sorry . . . children," he managed.

"That's better," said Calvert. "And I'll see you in Giraffe Class tomorrow morning at ten sharp to review our Giraffe Fundamentals. Now have fun, kids!" He waved dumbly and walked off.

"Bye!" they yelled.

Darren sighed and tried to make peace with the birthday boy. "Okay, okay, how much mustard do you want on your—" The boy stomped on his foot once more. "Aaaaaahheeeeeeee!" cried Darren. The kids guffawed.

AT HIS FIRST AND ONLY BREAK, Darren rushed out to the back parking lot and called Jamie on his cell phone.

"Did you show your boss the broom yet?" he asked hopefully.

Jamie was restocking greeting cards. "No, I haven't stopped working for a second here, dude. I'm like one a' them Oompa-Loompas."

"Come on, you have to do it today," pleaded Darren. "I've got to get out of here—the little brats are allowed to *attack* me now!"

"Okay, okay, I'm on it. Gotta go."

TEN MINUTES LATER, Mike approached Jamie, who was feverishly scrubbing the grill with a thick steel pad.

"When you finish that, I want you to clean the freezer," he said. "It's going to be a late day."

"Great! Thanks!" responded Jamie, oddly agreeable.

"Uh . . . you're welcome," Mike replied suspiciously.

"Oh, hey, man, I almost forgot—I've got something to show you."

"What?"

"It's an invention my friend Darren and I made."

"An invention?"

"Yeah, it's sort of a mechanical broom that . . . Hmm, how can I describe it? Oh, wait, I've got one right here!" Jamie reached behind a storage room door and wheeled out a large object, covered with a sheet. "You ready for this?" he said. He yanked the sheet away, revealing a very peculiar contraption. "Bam!" he barked, his arms outstretched.

It was, indeed, an elaborate mechanical broom. A small control box sat between a set of handlebars, which led down a thick shaft to a huge, heavy motor. The whole load rested on one back wheel and two larger front wheels. Stretched out between the front wheels was a long metal cylinder with ten small broom heads sticking out from it. Behind them trailed a wide red dustpan, ready to trap any dirt that came its way.

"What on earth is that?" said Mike.

"It's our all-new, three-speed, turbo-charged mechanical broom—the Super Sucker! They'll sell like crazy!"

"You mean *here?*"

"Well, yeah, we've got a whole mess of them all ready to go! This thing is really slammin,' man!"

"Oh, slamming, huh? Does it even work?"

"Are you kidding? It rocks!"

Jamie emptied a paper bag filled with garbage and lint onto the floor. Dust kicked up from the pile, which did little to amuse Mike.

"You think the iPod was a big deal?" said Jamie. "This'll sell twice as many."

He tripped a switch on the control box and the machine sprung to life, headlights blazing. The motor made a loud whirring sound as the broom heads spun around on the cylinder. Jamie pressed a button, moved the machine forward, and sure enough, the blur of brooms scooped the dirt into the dustpan. Some of the garbage blew out from the sides, but it was enough to impress Mike and a few customers who had gathered to watch.

"Hey, that thing's pretty neat," Mike admitted.

"And that's not even the best part, dude. Check out *this* action."

Jamie pressed another button, which kicked the motor into a higher, louder gear. He let go of the handlebars and the machine took off on its own, hunting for garbage. It hit a wall, nimbly spun around, and charged forward, continuing its quest.

Mike had to shout to be heard over the roaring motor. "Wow, look at that thing! It really works!"

"What?"

"I said it really—"

The Super Sucker suddenly emitted a sharp *bang*. Smoke shot out the back and the motor jumped to an even higher, earsplitting gear. The machine lurched out of control, attacking a stack of magazines and ripping them to shreds. A blizzard of confetti spewed into the air.

"Stop it, stop it!" Mike yelled. "It's gone berserk!"

A startled Jamie ran toward it, but the machine seemed to take on a life of its own. It zipped off to the left just as he reached out to grab the handlebars. He yelled as he tripped over the torn paper and flew into a stand of lipstick and nail polish. The entire display went *crashing* to the floor with him.

"Jamie, stop that thing!" screamed Mike as the frightened customers scattered. "Ah, forget it, I'll do it myself!"

The machine barreled about like an enraged bull. Mike strode toward it, and it charged right at him. He tried grabbing it, saying, "Come here, you little—" but the spinning brooms attacked his feet, drawing them underneath the broom heads. He tripped to the ground, and the mechanical mugger continued up Mike's legs, firmly trapping him. He struggled to free himself, his limbs flailing about wildly.

"Get this insane thing off of me!" he roared.

Jamie jumped up and dove at the machine, tackling it headlong. He flew into a revolving bookstand, which slammed into a huge glass display case, filled with fragile crystal figurines. The entire case slowly tilted over.

"*Noooooooooooooo!*" cried Mike helplessly as the case plunged to the floor. The crash that followed was heard down the block and would never be forgotten by all who witnessed it. The case narrowly missed two elderly nuns who sped out of the way just in time, one by burning rubber in her wheelchair.

The felled mechanical broom bellowed a desperate final growl and stopped dead with another thunderous *bang*. A cloud of exhaust billowed from its motor, completely enveloping Jamie and Mike. Mike coughed uncontrollably as he climbed up out of the smoke.

"What, are you trying to kill me?" he shouted.

"Dude, sorry!" said Jamie, stumbling to his feet. "I don't know how that happened."

"That thing is a dangerous weapon! Look at this place!" The place was undeniably in shambles.

"Wow. It always worked at Darren's house," assured Jamie.

"Darren? Is he the ring leader of the operation?"

"What? No, Darren Jackson, my best friend. I've known him since I was three, and we both—"

"Never mind! If I ever see that thing again, you'll be fired on the spot! Do you understand me?"

"Yeah, yeah, I'll, uh, I'll just take it out of here."

Jamie stood the machine up while Mike surveyed the damage. "My God," he said. "Who do you think is going to pay for all of this?"

"Uh . . . the insurance company?" hoped Jamie, but he could tell by the unpleasant look on Mike's face that he was mistaken. "Or, uh . . . me?"

"That would be correct, my friend. You can expect a smaller paycheck. Now clean this mess up!"

Jamie sighed. It certainly *was* going to be a late day, and he knew that Darren would be upset about the broom's complete failure.

It seemed to Jamie that he'd known Darren forever, but they became close when they both lost their fathers in the same week five years ago. Darren's father died suddenly, and Jamie's father ran off with a young, heavily tatooed barmaid, never to be heard from again. Even though the boys were very different, they jelled instantly, fitting together like pieces of a puzzle— Darren was smart, but not very popular, while Jamie was popular, but not very smart. Darren helped Jamie with schoolwork and Jamie helped Darren make more friends. Jamie would often greet him with, "Whassup, my brutha from another mutha!" followed by a man hug (which took Darren a while to get used to).

They also shared an interest in magic, and once tried putting on their own show. They didn't practice their tricks enough, however, and their botched attempt discouraged them from ever trying again. They decided to just work on getting rich so they could escape the feeling of hopelessness their lower-class Washington suburb instilled in them. It wasn't only for themselves—they often discussed being able to help their mothers have easier, carefree lives. Jamie was happy to follow Darren's lead and help however he could.

At the moment, though, there was a huge mess to straighten up and a freezer to clean. Jamie, resigned to his fate, shrugged and got to work.

CHAPTER 2

The New Road to Riches

"OH, MAN, it *attacked* him?" Darren couldn't believe his ears. Even worse, he couldn't understand why Jamie found it so darned funny. The two stood in Jamie's kitchen, eating bowls of green Jell-O, and cookies freshly baked by Jamie's mother, Marie. Jamie's Boston Terrier, Maxwell, sniffed the bent and busted mechanical broom, which sat innocently nearby.

"You should have seen it!" exclaimed Jamie, doubling over with laughter. "It had my boss pinned to the ground, and it was just beatin' on him! No mercy!"

"Man, that's not cool!" said Darren. "We've got eighteen of these things sittin' downstairs. How are we ever going to sell them now?"

"Listen," said Marie, rinsing off cookie sheets while brushing back her tangled mass of curly brown hair, "I think it's great that you were able to make those things at all. But now it's time for you boys to concentrate on your school work so you can get into good colleges."

"Momma, college is good, but it doesn't always make you rich," replied Jamie.

"Don't tell any rich person that," Marie countered. "Most of them have college degrees."

"Oh, yeah?" said Jamie. "What about George Washington? He never went to college."

"Was he rich?" asked Darren.

"Are you kidding?" said Jamie. "He's got his photo ID on everybody's money!"

Marie and Darren shook their heads. They were used to Jamie's twisted logic, and they mostly let it slide. (Marie's ex-husband, a truck driver, once told her their son was stupid, and she said, "He's not stupid. He just dances to his own tune." "Yeah, right," said his father. "Looney Tunes.")

Marie picked up a kitchen rag. "Being rich isn't everything, anyway. There's more to life than being rich, you know."

"Yeah, you're right," said Jamie. "There's being rich . . . and being famous, too!"

Darren laughed. "Yeah, you got it!"

"Come on, Darren," said Jamie, scarfing down the last of his Jell-O. "Let's go figure out why that heap went all Terminator on us. Thanks for the goodies, Mama."

"Yeah, thanks, Mrs. Jenks," added Darren.

Jamie planted a big kiss on his mother's cheek, causing her to giggle. He grabbed the bowl of cookies.

"Hey, leave those here," said Marie. "You can't eat them all at once."

"Wanna bet?" he joked, returning the bowl. He scooped up two, then a third, and he and Darren headed downstairs with the mechanical broom. Maxwell barked and followed them down.

"Now don't make a big mess down there again!" Marie called out, and she shook her head and wiped her cheek. She looked around at her small, old kitchen. Okay, she wasn't rich, she thought, or thin and beautiful anymore, for that matter, but she had a loving son, her cashier job at the supermarket, and her health—the rest was icing. She took a bite of a warm cookie. "Oh, yeah," she cooed. She closed her eyes and thought *It doesn't get much better than this.*

JAMIE AND DARREN dissected the broom piece by piece. Three rows of Super Sucker machines were neatly lined up against the back wall of the tidy basement, looking like robotic soldiers ready for action. Behind them, an old TV aired cartoons.

"Ah, it was the stupid motor," said Darren, throwing down a screwdriver in disgust. "I knew we shouldn't have used more than three hundred volts."

"But you said we needed all that to move it *and* spin the brooms," said Jamie, collecting the scattered screws and bolts.

"Yeah, and now it attacks people! It's Sephiroth on

wheels! Oh, man, we spent almost all of our savings on these things."

They sighed as Jamie's attention wandered to the cartoon on TV. "Oh, look, it's The Cave Squirrels! I love them!"

Two squirrels, dressed as a caveman and cavewoman, faced a gang of mean-looking beavers. The beavers' leader had spiky fur, tattoos, and a wide jaw that jutted out from his face. "I told you this was *our* forest, squirrels!" he growled. "You have one minute to get out of town, or else!"

The other beavers, wielding sharpened tree limbs, geared up for battle.

"I think we're ready to *go* to town," replied the male squirrel, lifting a large wooden club into batting position.

"Get 'im, Sparky!" yelled the female squirrel.

He swung the club at the beaver, and *smack*—it whacked him hard, sending him high in the air. He landed on his feet in a daze. The female squirrel wound up her own club and rammed the beaver in the legs. He did mid-air flips as smoke shot out around him, his body a spinning blur. He landed with a *thud* against a tree, and colorful cartoon birdies appeared, circling his head with *tweet-tweets* and *cuckoos*. The other beavers, frightened by the display, dropped their weapons and fled.

"Go, Cave Squirrels!" said Jamie, laughing.

"Okay, that is the lamest show there ever was," chided Darren, picking up the TV remote.

"Hey, I'm watching that!"

"Not anymore," said Darren.

He turned the channel—a magician was performing illusions on a talk show.

"Hey, look, it's The Amazing Ozlo!" said Jamie, just as happy to see this instead.

They watched the magician, a slick, handsome guy, about thirty-five, with long, straight dark hair, dressed in a snappy black and silver outfit. He leaped atop a wooden trunk, which was bound with chains. He held up a shimmering red cloth, shielding himself from view, and *fwoosh*—the cloth was ripped in two by his beautiful female assistant who now stood on the trunk in his place. The magician was gone.

"Wow, did you see that?" exclaimed Jamie.

"*Way* cool."

On TV, two assistants unchained the trunk and lifted the lid, revealing a canvas bag. They untied the bag, and the magician stepped out, locked in handcuffs. He also sported a completely new outfit, covered with sparkly purple sequins.

"How did he get locked in that trunk so fast?" wondered Darren.

"Yeah, and he changed his clothes, too!" marveled Jamie. "How did he change his clothes?"

"What? The clothes were easy, man. He must have had that outfit on underneath the first one."

"Nah, look how shiny it is—you would have seen it through the other one."

Darren ignored this.

The Amazing Ozlo bowed to his very enthusiastic audience and kissed his shapely blond assistant. She wrapped her arms around him, kicked up a leg, and displayed a toothy smile.

"He's dating that model," said Jamie. "Man, she's blazin'! He is so lucky."

"It's not luck, man. The guy's rich. Of *course* she likes him."

"Yeah, I'll bet he's got a million dollars."

"A million? The guy's got a giant mansion in Beverly Hills and private jets and everything. He's gotta be a gazillionaire!"

"Yeah, right? Sweet!"

Wheels suddenly churned in Darren's head. "Hey . . . Jamie."

"What?"

"I have an idea. I mean a really big idea. What does that guy have that we don't have?"

"A gazillion bucks and a cracklin' hot girlfriend."

"Exactly!"

Jamie thought for a moment. "Did I miss something?"

"Don't you see? He's got all that because of his magic. Remember that time we put on a magic show for your family picnic?"

"Yeah, even my Great Aunt Charlotte said we sucked."

"But that was four years ago, and we didn't really rehearse the tricks first."

"Yeah? So?"

"So, now that we're older, we can really kick some butt! And we'll add new stuff, too. We'll be the hot new magic duo! We'll call ourselves, uh, Jackson and Jenks. We'll be huge!"

"Ah, I see. But dude, how come, automatically, your name's going first? I mean how come it's not Jenks and Jackson?"

"Uh, well that would be your, you know, alphabetical order," he reasoned.

Jamie thought for a few seconds. And a few seconds more. "Oh," he said finally.

Darren excitedly paced about the room. "Now listen, we'll start off small. Then once we take off, we'll get lions and stuff, just like Ozlo."

"You really think we can do it?"

"Don't you?"

"No."

"Well, we can! We just have to work at it this time. I swear to you, Jamie—two years from now, we're gonna be famous magicians. They'll put our names in lights! Then it'll be Maseratis and mansions and private jets and all the babes you can—"

"Do you think I'll be able to get a pony?"

"A pony?"

"Yeah, I always wanted a pony—a little pretty one."

Darren wondered why Jamie wanted a pony, but not wanting to ruin the moment, he exclaimed, "Yes, you will get that pony!"

"Well, dude, all right, then! Cool!"

"Bring it on!"

The two launched into an overhead hand slap and shouted, "Deeeal!" Maxwell barked and jumped, begging to be part of the fun. Jamie laughed and scratched his dog's ears.

CHAPTER 3

Magic vs. Maxwell

THAT WEEKEND, Jamie dug up their old magic tricks and books from his garage. They picked up scrap lumber from a construction site and had a great time sawing, nailing, and painting a large trunk, very much like the one they'd seen on TV. They also put together a levitation trick they'd found in Darren's old *Cub Scout Handbook.* After two weeks of building and rehearsing, their act was prepared. They couldn't wait to perform their new show.

The next Friday at five o'clock, kids crammed into Jamie's garage, quickly grabbing seats on chairs, old mattresses, and bedspreads. They eagerly anticipated the "Wondrous Feats of Magic and Illusion" promised them by the flyers the boys had posted around the neighborhood. Maxwell scampered about, gleefully accepting plentiful petting and attention.

Darren stood outside collecting the fifty-cent admission fee. "Step right up, kids! No one turned away!"

With everyone seated, Darren and Jamie stepped onto a wide wooden platform they'd built.

"Ladies and gentlemen, boys and girls!" announced Darren. "Today, you'll be seeing wondrous illusions performed by the one, the only magic team of Jackson and Jenks!" A few kids clapped, the rest just stared. "I'm Darren Jackson and this is my partner, Jamie Jenks! And now, without any further ado, we begin the magic."

Jamie displayed a section from a newspaper as Darren said, "My partner, as you can plainly see, is holding a common household newspaper."

"Yes," said Jamie, "and now I will fold this very newspaper into a cone-like shape, like this."

He folded the paper while, unseen by the audience, he slipped a clear plastic tube from his sleeve into the bottom of the cone. The tube ran underneath his shirt and pants, and down through a hole in the platform.

Darren picked up a large glass pitcher of milk and said, "Now watch as we make the milk disappear into thin air. Are you ready, Amazing Jamie?"

"Ready and waiting, Dynamic Darren."

Darren poured the milk into the cone. The milk slid down the hidden tube and into a container below the platform. All was going according to plan, but Darren was pouring too fast. The milk, unable to seep into the tube fast enough, was quickly rising to the top the newspaper.

"Wait, slow down a bit, Darren," Jamie pleaded.

Darren, not seeing the problem, just continued pouring, saying, "Now, in just a second, we will see if we can—"

The cone burst open. "Aaaaaaah!" cried Jamie as the milk gushed free, splashing about and drenching the floor.

"Look what you did!" yelled Darren over the children's peals of laughter.

"You wouldn't stop pouring!" said Jamie. "Oh, man, look at that!" He pointed to Darren's sopping wet pants, causing more laughter from the kids.

"Oh, great!"

"I told you to slow down!" said Jamie, walking toward Darren to help clean him up.

"No, don't move!" hollered Darren, but it was too late. The hidden tube, attached to the floor, ripped from Jamie's pants.

"Oh, bonk!" yelled Jamie, realizing he'd exposed the trick.

The tube flopped about, milk spewing forth. Darren grabbed its end—the milk shot into his face. "Baaaaaah!" he yelled as the kids fell all over themselves, weak with laughter. "All right, all right, kids," he pleaded. "Just calm down, calm down now. We have a lot more tricks to show you, some of which might actually work." He glared hard at Jamie while wiping his face and pants with a scarf.

The laughter subsided and Darren continued. "Now, for our next trick, I am going to make Jamie float in the air. It's a feat I'm sure you will all remember for the rest of your natural lives."

The two lifted a bench onto the platform and Jamie lay on it face up. "Darren will now place a cloth over me."

"Yes, here now is the cloth that I will place over the Amazing Jamie," confirmed Darren. He draped an old blue bed sheet over Jamie's body, leaving only his head uncovered. The remainder of the sheet lay bunched up on the platform.

Unseen behind the cloth, Darren handed Jamie a set of fake legs, made from pieces of broomsticks that were covered with pant legs and sneakers which matched the ones Jamie was wearing. Jamie grabbed onto the legs, one in each hand, and held them outstretched underneath the cloth. He moved his real feet to the floor behind the bench. Darren then pulled back the sheet revealing the fake legs and feet. With Jamie's head sticking out from one end of the sheet and the fake feet sticking out from the other, everything looked normal; Jamie's outstretched arms appeared to be his body underneath the cloth.

"Okay!" said a pleased Darren, waving his hand over Jamie. "Now, for the incredible illusion—Jamie's body will grow lighter and lighter. Do you feel any lighter yet, Amazing Jamie?"

"Yes, I do, Dynamic Darren. And now, I will rise!"

Jamie slowly stood up with his head tilted back underneath the cloth. With his arms holding the fake legs in front of him, he appeared to be floating in the air.

"Riiiiiiiiise," said Jamie eerily, as if in a trance.

"Wow!" the kids gasped.

"There you have it," announced Darren. "Jackson and Jenks's Floating Man!"

The crowd applauded, truly mystified. Just then, however, Maxwell ran up, bit down on the cloth, and yanked on it.

"Maxwell! Nooooo!" shouted Darren, but the determined dog pulled the sheet away entirely, revealing Jamie standing there, holding the fake legs. The audience rocked with laughter once again, gleefully pointing and shouting.

Darren panicked. He tried to throw the cloth back over Jamie, but was stopped by Maxwell, who began a spirited game of tug of war. The small, but strong dog proved a formidable opponent as he growled and pulled with all his might.

"Give me that, you little . . . !"

The sheet ripped in two, and Maxwell ran off with his half. Their second trick was exposed, and the kids were beside themselves, teary with laughter.

Jamie, trying to make the best of the situation, used the fake legs to enact a tap dance. "Ink, a-dink-a-doo, a-dink-a-doo!" he sang. The kids were amused, but not Darren.

"Okay, that's enough of that, uh, Amazing Jamie. . . . Stop it, you wingnut!" Jamie halted the routine. "Well, we seem to have run into, uh, some technical difficulty with that last trick," Darren gamely continued, "but I'm sure this next illusion will have you all feeling amazed and spellbound."

Darren and Jamie hauled the wooden trunk onto the platform and performed their version of The Amazing Ozlo's locked box trick. Jamie tied Darren's hands with rope, and

Darren climbed into the trunk. Jamie shut the lid and sealed it with a padlock. He then stood on top of the trunk and held a large red cloth outstretched up to his neck, covering his body and the trunk itself.

"Watch!" announced Jamie. "I will count to five, and something truly amazing will occur!" He raised the cloth high above his head.

Unseen by the audience, there was a gaping hole in back of the trunk for Darren to escape through. Huffing and puffing, he slid his paunchy body out of the hole.

"Here we go!" said Jamie. "One! Two!" Darren climbed onto the trunk behind him. "Three! Four!"

Darren grasped the cloth just as Jamie released it. Their combined weight, however, was too much for the rickety lid to handle. Just as Darren yelled "Five!" the lid split in half, and the two plunged through it. The cloth sailed down on top of them, and they wriggled, flailed, and fought to free themselves. The kids, as was now a matter of routine, convulsed with laughter.

AS THE AUDIENCE milled out of the garage a short time later, Darren and Jamie gave each of them their fifty cents back.

"There you go, young lady," said Darren to the last child. "Go buy yourself an ice cream or something."

"Keep the change," the girl needled. "Go buy yourself some better tricks or something!" She and her friends laughed and ran off.

"Go buy yourself some better tricks or something," Darren mockingly mimicked. "Well, that whole show was— hmm, let's see—a total bust!"

"It didn't go too well," said Jamie plainly.

"No, it didn't go too well! It was pathetic! All that work, and that was the best we could do!"

Jamie thought for a second. "Too bad we didn't have a lion, like the Amazing Ozlo."

"Yeah, sure, a lion would have helped!" He addressed the empty seats. "You want to laugh at us, kids? Take it up with the kitty cat!" He groaned and collapsed in a chair. "Oh, man, I wanted us to be the best magicians in the world. Instead, we're the worst who ever walked the face of the earth."

"Well, now *that's* something," said Jamie, apparently finding a bright side. "Not many people can say *that*."

Darren shook his head sadly.

THE NEXT DAY at Jimmy Giraffe's was pandemonium for Darren—there were more children than usual, as well as a smaller waiting staff. Darren deflected a speeding five-year-old from ramming him full force as he lowered a large pepperoni pizza onto a table.

"There you go," he said to a horde of hungry six-year-olds. "Dig in."

A sea of hands tore at the feast as Darren's cell phone rang. He looked around for Calvert, whose exuberant passion for reviewing Giraffe Fundamentals struck Darren as being a little twisted. Seeing no sign of him, he grabbed his phone, saw that it was Jamie, and answered it.

"Can't take calls while I'm working, Holmes. Giraffe Fundamental Number Seven-B."

Jamie was at the convenience store, hiding out in the storage room. "We got a job!" he said in a loud whisper.

"What?" replied Darren. "I can't hear you."

"We got a job, man! A magic show!"

"Are you kidding me?"

"No! My mother just called. Remember old Mr. Dooley, the elementary school principal? He wants us to do a show for the school's closing assembly."

"Shut up! Really?" exclaimed Darren.

"Yeah. He said the kids told him we were the funniest magicians they ever saw."

"Funniest? Well, whatever. Is he going to pay us?"

"Yeah! Two hundred dollars!"

"Two hundred dollars?" shouted Darren, and he added a phrase his mother said whenever she was excited: "Get off the phone!"

Jamie hung up.

CHAPTER 4

Zoltrad Awakens

BACK IN JAMIE'S BASEMENT, Darren called Principal Dooley and arranged a performance for the students' last day of school. The timing was right—Darren and Jamie's sophomore year would end two days earlier. They proceeded to rethink and retool the act.

A week later, Darren hammered the last nail into a new, sturdier lid for the locked trunk illusion. Jamie climbed on top to test it.

"Darren, remember when The Amazing Ozlo did this trick? He came out wearing a different outfit."

"So?"

"So *we* should do that. When I come out, I should be wearing, like, a scuba outfit. Wouldn't that be stellar?"

"No, it wouldn't," said Darren, wiping sawdust off the trunk. "But what if you came out in something magical, like, uh, like a wizard outfit?"

"Yeah, a wizard outfit! But where are we going to get one of those?"

AN HOUR LATER, the boys climbed off a city bus and entered the enormous Salvation Army Thrift Shop in the middle of the town's bustling business district.

"Wow," exclaimed Jamie, taking in the endless rows of used clothing, appliances, toys, books, and knick-knacks. "How do you find anything in here?"

"You look around. Come on."

An employee with "Lindsay" on her nametag approached them. She wore jeans and a T-shirt, which read *I'm Also the President of IBM*. Behind her geeky, retro glasses, Darren thought, she's pretty cute. She looked to be in her late teens and had nose freckles and red hair in a pigtail.

"Hi, can I help you?" she asked sweetly.

"Yeah, hi," said Darren. "We're looking for something in a, you know, like a, umm . . ."

"We need a wizard outfit!" helped Jamie.

"A wizard outfit," said Lindsay, amused. "Wow, which one of you is the real Harry Potter?"

"Oh, heh, heh," offered Darren. "No, we're magicians. The costume is for our act." He was quite taken with the comely Lindsay.

"We're Jackson and Jenks," announced Jamie. "Have you heard of us?"

"Umm, no, can't say that I have."

"Well, we haven't really done any magic yet, is probably why," said Darren, giving Jamie a sideways sneer.

"Yes, that's probably it," giggled Lindsay.

"Uh, I'm Darren and this is Jamie."

"Lindsay Cranford," she said, and they shook hands.

"Ah. Good," said Darren, unable to think of anything flirty to say. "So, uh, do you have anything like that? Costumes, I mean?"

"Well, if you head to the costume racks in back to the left, you might find something. I can't make any promises, though."

"No, that's fine. Thanks, Lindsay," said Darren.

"Sure," she said, flashing a glowing smile. "Good luck."

The two headed to the back. "You thought she was hot, didn't you?" teased Jamie.

"Who . . . her?"

"Yeah, come on, admit it! You could hardly talk around her!" He cackled and gave Darren a friendly punch on the shoulder.

"Cut it out, man. All right, she was okay."

"Hey, why don't you ask her out on a date? Maybe then you'd finally be able to say that you kissed a girl."

"Hey, shut up, okay?" snapped Darren. "I've kissed lots of girls."

"Yeah? When?"

"I kissed Cindy Carr in the woods that time, or don't you remember?"

"You said she didn't kiss you back."

"Could *I* help it? Look, when you're shootin' for your first million, girls just get in the way. You know what I'm saying?"

"Yeah, you're afraid of girls."

"What? I'm not afraid of—oh, forget it. There's the costumes. Come on."

The boys combed through endless rows of Bugs Bunny, Batman, and Frankenstein outfits, but they weren't finding anything remotely wizardly. Jamie grabbed up a rubber mask of the President of the United States and pulled it over his head.

"Look, Darren, I'm President Brady!" He waved his hands about. "Hello, Americans! Helloooooooo!"

"Yeah, that's not *too* dorky. Come on, help me look for this thing."

Jamie returned the mask and spotted an old yellow cardboard box on the floor, underneath a row of pants. He slid the box out and combed through its contents. There was a woodcarving of a hideous face, a dirty triangular pendant, a faded green maraca, and a corroded antique brass bottle. He looked about for Darren, who had moved an aisle away.

"Hey, Darren, come look at this!"

"You found wizard stuff?"

"No, but this is really cool."

"Forget it, man—just keep looking. I don't want to be in this place all day. It smells all crusty in here."

Jamie picked up the brass bottle and examined it. Its wide

mouth led down to a thin neck, then ballooned out like a ball at its base. Dark red rivets dressed its ornate neck design, and it bore an inscription that was covered with dirt and dust. Jamie blew off the dust, but the letters were still illegible. He rubbed the bottle, cleaning it, but he still couldn't read it. He rubbed harder—no luck. Giving up, he returned the bottle and kicked the box back under the pants rack. He continued sifting through the costumes.

Then it happened.

Unseen by Jamie, a clear, shapeless cloud oozed up and out from inside the bottle. It moved slowly at first and grew larger, shifting about. The undulating orb hung in the air, constantly changing directions as if searching for something. Suddenly, it disappeared.

Just then, another customer tried passing behind Jamie. He was a sharply dressed, gray-haired businessman in his late forties. He chatted on a cell phone as Jamie scooted forward to let him by.

"Why, of course, Emily, darling," said the man. "Yes, Daddy will get you the best costume in the world, I promise. . . . A duck outfit, yes. Listen, would you stop crying? I'm in the store now. . . . Please stop crying, Emily, honey, I'll get you the outfit. . . . Emily, I'll see you very soon. Bye-bye." He hung up and thumbed through the costumes.

In a flash, the bubble reappeared behind the man and rapidly grew to his size. Then, without a sound, it flew right at him. He seemed completely unfazed as the orb zapped itself into his body. Instantly, he froze in his tracks. His body straightened and his eyes popped open wide. He turned toward Jamie, who, examining a shiny jacket, had missed the whole event.

"Hello!" said the man in a bold voice.

A surprised Jamie eyed him strangely and returned an equally bold "Hello!"

The man looked around as if experiencing his surroundings for the first time. "Where are we, please?" he asked, still rather loudly.

"Excuse me?"

"This place. What is this, and where?"

Jamie was confused, but played along with the man's odd game. "Last I checked, it's a thrift shop in Washington, D.C."

"D.C.," the man repeated.

Jamie, a little worried, tried to dismiss him. "Yeah. Uh-huh. Okay." He resumed his search and began humming.

The man cleared his throat. "I am Zoltrad from the Calysto Galaxy. I am commonly known as a genie. You have three wishes." Jamie ignored him, but the man continued. "First, though, there are three rules involved. Rule number one: You can't wish for money."

Jamie hummed louder and sang, "Lookin'. Lookin' through the costumes. Many fine costumes to look through here."

Darren overheard the customer and listened from behind a rack.

"Rule number two: The wishing powers can be transferred

to somebody else, but only if the current bearer of the wishes requests that to happen. And he must request it out loud, so that I can hear it. Do you understand?"

Jamie sensed the conclusion of the man's speech. "Yeah, uh-huh, transferring the wishin' powers. Very important, good to know."

"And the last rule: My bottle is the only thing in the world that can't be moved, changed, or vanished with a wish."

"No movin' the bottle."

"Good. What is your first wish?"

Darren suddenly grabbed Jamie's arm and whisked him away. "Gotta go, important meeting, must leave immediately."

"A meeting?" said Jamie. "Okay. Bye, genie-guy. Peace!"

"No, wait!" the man pleaded. "You have three wishes! Come with me and you can have whatever you want! Anything at all!"

"He wishes you'd leave him alone! How about that?" said Darren as the two hurried out. "Ya freak," he murmured.

"Darren, what's the meeting about?" asked Jamie, opening the front door.

"It's about why you would stand there listening to a crazy whacko who says he's a genie!"

The man-turned-genie watched blankly as the two left the store. He then straightened up and froze, and the clear, heaving orb zipped out of him. It hovered in the air, and, with a quiet snap, it disappeared.

The man's body shuddered, and, once again a normal

customer, he looked around, a bit confused. The boy next to him seemed to have vanished. But no matter—he had to find a costume for his daughter, and he continued the search.

THE BOYS walked a few blocks and entered Mosi's Deli, their favorite small diner. They had been customers for so long that the owner, Mosi Davis, thought of them as family. Mosi was an elderly black man, balding and slightly hunched over, and the boys often helped him, free of charge, with whatever he needed: moving boxes, making deliveries, and standing in as sandwich makers whenever he was short-handed. The two always looked forward to seeing Mosi and joking around with him.

The last customer left shortly after the boys arrived. Now able to relax, Mosi examined a sheet of lottery tickets while Darren moved crates of pickle jars. Jamie stood tiptoe on the counter, smacking an ancient television set in hopes of tuning it in.

"Come on, TV!" *Smack.* "I know you can do it, don't give up on me now!" *Smack.* Suddenly, the picture came in clearly. "Bam! You see that?" The signal then faded, leaving static. "Ahhhh! You're playin' with me now, TV! Are you playin' with me now? Bring it on, you dumb old crate!"

"Gonna win this gol-darn thing this time," declared Mosi, showing Darren his lottery tickets. "It's ten thousand dollars a week for life, can you imagine that? Wonder what I'm gonna do with all that money." He emitted a raspy, wheezing cackle.

"What *are* you going to do with it, Mosi?" humored Darren. "You gonna fly to Miami and chase women on the beach?"

"Nah, are you kiddin'? I'm gonna fly to the *French Riviera* and chase women on the beach!" He cackled again, louder and harder, which sounded only slightly more painful. "But you know what I'd really do with the money?"

"What?" asked Darren.

"I'd put half away every week, and I'd give the other half to you boys."

"Really?" chirped Darren and Jamie in unison.

"Yeah, and I wouldn't even think about telling my ol' wife about it. Her and her family been eatin' me dry ever since I'm twenty-five years old. I've had two heart attacks in my day, and it's thanks to that family, the whole stinkin' lot of 'em. But you two been comin' here and helpin' me for years—ain't never asked nothin' for it. Yessuh, I'd give half of it to you."

"Aw, that's a really nice thought, Mosi," said Darren.

"I wish you *would* win the lottery, Mosi," said Jamie, giving the TV another smack. "Maybe you'd buy a new TV and—"

Without warning, a howling burst of wind *exploded* through the rickety front door, which slammed hard against the wall. The gust blew violently with a whooshing whistle as the three fought to steady themselves. Jamie grabbed onto the metal brackets holding the TV and hung on, his feet dangling, while Darren and Mosi hugged the counters.

Then, just as quickly, there was an eerie silence and dead

calm. The three were frozen in shock until Jamie exclaimed, *"Off the freakin' hook!"* He dropped back to the counter and climbed down.

"What was up with *that?*" said Darren in disbelief.

"Must be the winds kickin' up from the ocean," reasoned Mosi, "but I ain't seen nothin' like that in ninety-two years of livin.' The weather's changin' every day, I tell ya. Never know what's gonna be."

Darren checked the front door, which was damaged from the wind's force. "We'll be needing some new hinges here, Mosi. Got any in back?"

"I might just, you know? Let me check right handy." Mosi shuffled toward the back. "Yessuh, you never know *what's* gonna happen these days."

Once he was gone, Darren and Jamie exchanged worried glances. When each realized that the other had been scared out of their gourds, they pointed and made fun of each other, laughing.

"You were like this, dawg—look, look!" Jamie made a grotesque face and waved his hands in the air while squealing.

"Yeah, but *you* were like *this . . ."* Darren swung from a shelf, acting like a frightened monkey. They continued teasing each other, chortling.

Mystified Magicians

ON THEIR FIRST DAY of summer vacation, the boys rehearsed a new trick in the basement while a news program played quietly on the TV. Jamie's mischievous dog, Maxwell, was now officially added to the act, and he seemed happy and eager to help. The trick: They would place Maxwell in a box and drape a shiny purple cloth over him. They'd then yank off the cloth and rip the box apart, showing that he had vanished.

Darren showed Jamie how the trick worked. The dog was secretly tucked into a cloth bag inside the box; the bag's material was an exact match of the purple cloth that would cover the box. When the box was ripped apart, Darren would secretly whisk the bag, with the dog, away with the cloth. The purple bag would blend in with the purple cloth, making it nearly invisible. After a few rehearsals, the trick was working great.

"Golden, dude!" said Jamie. "This one's gonna rock 'em!"

"Yeah, as long as your dog doesn't mess us up again."

"Oh, he'll be cool. Won't you, Maxwell?" He pet Maxwell, who offered reassuring licks.

On TV, a handsome anchorman announced, "Well, there's a new winner of the 'Ten Thousand a Week for Life' lottery game today. Let's go live to Lottery Headquarters where the owner of a small downtown deli has stepped forward to claim his prize."

The boys gasped and ran to the TV. Darren turned up the volume as the anchorman continued.

"The ticket holder is Mosi Davis, who's ninety-two years young and still going strong."

"He won!" Jamie shouted.

"There he is!" said Darren.

A battery of cameras and reporters crowded Mosi as he stood behind a podium. "I knew I was going to win when I bought the tickets yesterday," he explained. "I even said it out loud. I said, 'This is my turn, dad-gummit! I'm winnin' the lottery.'"

Jamie and Darren broke out screaming and shouting, "He won! He won!" Then it hit them—"We get half! We get half! We're rich! We're rich!"

Darren couldn't contain himself. "That's five thousand dollars a week for life! Five thousand dollars—every single week!"

"Hoo-weeee!" said Jamie.

"We'll never have to work again! Not ever!" The boys grabbed each other and jumped up and down. "We're rich, we're rich, we're rich, rich, rich!"

In their excitement, they missed what was happening on TV—Mosi suddenly grasped his chest and keeled over. Pandemonium ensued as people rushed in to help. Some screamed, some shouted for a doctor.

"We're rich, we're . . . Wait, hold on, man," said Darren.

The duo watched, and their faces fell. People ran to Mosi as the camera dug in for a close-up. He was not looking good.

"Mosi!" cried Darren.

MOSI had a simple funeral. About twenty people surrounded the casket for the burial ceremony. A somber Jamie and Darren, in dark jackets and ties, stood watching.

"He was a great guy," said Jamie sadly. "I'm really going to miss him."

"Yeah, me, too," added Darren quietly. "Funny old Mosi."

Darren tried to secretly wipe a tear from his eye by pretending a speck of dust had lodged there.

"Are you . . . crying?" asked Jamie.

"What?" piped Darren, jerking his hand from his face. "No, man, I never . . ." He noticed a bit of wetness under Jamie's eyes. "Are *you* crying?"

"Me? *No*, I'm just, uh . . . Your tie's crooked."

"Oh."

As Darren straightened his tie, Jamie quickly wiped his eyes. Darren then reached into his jacket pocket and pulled out a small bag of tissues. He silently handed one to Jamie and took one for himself. They dabbed their eyes and sniffled.

Mosi's wife stood quietly with her family. The minister said, "Mosi was a good man, beloved by all. It was one of life's great ironies that he won the 'Ten Thousand a Week for Life' lottery just before the Lord came for him. So he won't collect any of the money, but—"

Mosi's wife started crying. Her daughter consoled her, and the minister continued.

"So he won't collect any of the money, but . . . "

"Nooooooooooo!" Mosi's wife dropped to her knees, sobbing. "No moneeeeey!" No moneeeeeeey!" She pounded the ground with her fists.

"Mother! Get ahold of yourself!" her daugher said as family members rushed in to help.

"Ten thousand a week for life, oh, ho, ho, ho, noooooo!"

Darren and Jamie exchanged shocked glances, shook their heads, and slowly turned to leave.

THE MAGIC SHOW for the elementary school started off well, but, despite their best efforts, it was looking like another dud for the duo. They performed the trunk illusion, and, as rehearsed, Darren was locked inside. Jamie stood atop the new lid and held out a large red cloth, which unfurled to the floor.

"Watch now as Jackson and Jenks perform the most amazing feat you'll ever see!" he announced. Darren crawled out of the hole, climbed onto the lid, and crouched behind Jamie. "One —two—three!" yelled Jamie, and he stooped down as Darren grasped the cloth and lowered it to reveal only himself.

"It's me!" Darren shouted proudly.

Jamie tried to sneak to the back by ducking between Darren's legs. He didn't crouch low enough, however, and he knocked Darren's feet out from under him. Darren tumbled backward off the trunk. "Eeyaaaaaaaah!" he yelled, taking the cloth with him.

Jamie was left crouching atop the trunk, uncovered. "Ah, bonk!" he said, disappointed.

The audience, as before, laughed uproariously at the team's failure. The boys scrambled to their feet and tried to move on with the show. This audience, however, was ruder than the last.

"Can't you do anything right?" heckled one kid.

"You're a couple of boneheads!" delivered another.

A boy in the front row shouted, "If you're real magicians, why don't you disappear?"

Jamie finally lost his cool. "I wish I *was* a real magician, dude," he snarled. "The first thing I'd do is make *you* disa—"

Instantly, two sets of heavy double doors in back of the auditorium slammed open with a solid *crack,* and a gale wind burst in with violent, deafening force. The kids and teachers let out startled shouts as the gusting torrent swept through the room and onto the stage.

Darren managed to eke out, "What the . . . ?" before he and Jamie covered their faces and fought to remain standing.

Scarves and tricks flew about and tables toppled.

Suddenly, the wind ceased. The kids shouted and wriggled excitedly in their seats, trying to figure out what happened. Darren and Jamie looked at each other, quite alarmed—this was an exact repeat of the windstorm in Mosi's Deli.

The paunchy, bespectacled school principal strode to the front, a bit shaken. "All right, kids! All right!" he said, calming everyone down, himself included. "There's nothing to be alarmed about, nothing at all. That was just, uh, a strong bit of breeze, nothing more to it. I guess, uh, our magicians were more magical than I thought." He chuckled weakly, and alone. "Anyway, it's over and I'm sure the boys have a few more tricks, so let's watch them closely. They're incredibly clever and amazing, aren't they? Let's give them a hand," he said, exiting to the back. But the kids, already unimpressed with the act, were now anxious and distracted as well.

"Okay, guys," said Darren in a nervous recovery mode. In spite of the bizarre wind, he was determined to save the show from ruin. "We do have a few more tricks as, uh, Mr. Dooley mentioned, and I think you will be quite amazed by what happens to Jamie's dog, uh, Maxwell."

Jamie led his dog out on a leash, and the crowd's attention refocused as they oohed and aahed at the animal, who wore a bright red bow around his neck.

"Now get ready as we perform the incredible vanishing dog trick!" said Darren.

Jamie removed Maxwell's leash and picked him up. "Wave

goodbye to the crowd, Maxwell," he said. He pumped Maxwell's paw, and the kids aaaaahed again while Darren opened the lid of the red box. Jamie lowered the dog into it and, secretly, into the purple bag hidden inside. Darren shut the lid and draped the purple cloth over it. They lifted the box off its table, each holding onto one side.

"Watch!" yelled Jamie, waving his hand. "Vanish, Maxwell! One—two—three!" Darren yanked the cloth away while Jamie tore the box apart. As promised, there was no dog. Jamie held up his hands, spouting "Ta-da!" but the kids weren't satisfied.

"Let's see under the cloth!" they yelled. Darren, worried, waved the edges of the cloth, hoping to appease the kids. "There's a bag there!" they continued, clearly not the least bit fooled. They chanted, "Open the bag! Open the bag! Open the bag! Open the bag!"

Flustered, Darren said, "Bag? There's no—" In his panic, he knocked into the table, and the bag dropped to the floor with a hideous *thud.*

"Maxwell!" yelled an alarmed Jamie. The kids laughed anew at the boys' fumbling. Jamie grabbed the bag and opened it, hoping to save his pet. What he saw surprised the audience and the magicians as well.

Maxwell was gone.

Jamie looked at Darren, aghast. *"Where's my dog?"* he cried.

Darren was at a loss, but didn't want to let the audience in on the problem. "It, uh, it vanished. . . . Yeah, it vanished!" he said, and he raised his arms in triumph. The kids, now truly amazed, applauded wildly. Jamie stood frozen, but Darren grabbed his shoulder and made him bow along with him. They pressed on, pretending that all was fine, but their discomfort was obvious.

"For our, uh, last effect," tried Darren, "we will, uh, attempt to make Jamie, uh, float in the air. Uh . . . here goes."

The audience murmured while Jamie lay down on the bench. Darren covered him with the bedspread, and Jamie secretly put his feet on the floor and switched to the fake legs.

"You will, uh, you will not believe your very eyes," said Darren. "Watch as I make Jamie rise!"

"Riiiiiiiiiiise," drawled Jamie, in fake trance mode.

Darren waved his hand and waited for Jamie to lift himself up. But a strange feeling came over Darren—his body felt very light. This couldn't be, he thought, but yes, it was happening and . . . *he* began to rise instead of Jamie. He panicked as he looked about.

"What the . . . What? What *is* this?" he yelled.

Jamie, whose eyes were shut, didn't notice Darren's mysterious ascent, but the audience saw it quite clearly. They screamed with shock and delight as Darren rose further into the air.

"*Heeeeeeeeeey!*" Darren yelled in fright. Jamie opened his eyes and saw his friend way above him, continuing to rise toward the top of the stage curtain.

"Darren!" he shouted, jumping up and dropping the fake legs and cloth. "Darren, what are you doing up there?"

"I haven't the slightest idea! Help me! *Heeeeeeeeeeeelp!*"

"What should I do?"

"I don't know!"

Jamie turned to the audience. "Quick! Emergency! Somebody call nine-one-one!" But the amazed teachers, enjoying what they thought was playful humor, just laughed and applauded. "Call nine-one-one!" repeated Jamie.

Darren disappeared out of sight above the curtains, and the audience strained their necks to see him.

"Hold onto something!" yelled Jamie as Darren clunked his head on the ceiling.

"Ouch! Help me! Get a ladder!"

Jamie looked around. "I don't see one! Just come down!"

With that, Darren was plummeting to the stage. *"Yaaaaaah,"* he screamed as he reached out and grabbed the curtains. He got a firm grip, but the force of his fall caused them to tear. The entire curtain ripped from the rod and went plunging down with him. *"EeeAAAAAAAAAH!"*

He fell to the floor, well-cushioned by the thick folds of fallen curtains. A panicked Jamie ran to him while the audience fell all over themselves, weak with laughter. This was no doubt the best, funniest magic show they'd ever seen—probably the funniest show, period.

"Darren! Are you okay?"

"I'm fine, I'm fine. *What the heck is going on?*"

"I don't know, but let's take a bow and get out of here!"

Darren stumbled to his feet, and the two accepted a standing ovation.

"How'd we do that? *Where'd the dog go?*" Darren wondered aloud over the cheering and clapping.

"I don't know," said Jamie, "but I want him back! I want Maxwell back right now!"

Poof! A cloud of smoke billowed from the floor next to them, and Maxwell jumped out of it, barking.

"Maxwell!" Jamie yelled as the dog leapt into his arms.

The audience laughed at this added surprise and amplified their exultation. The duo faced front, forcing the biggest smiles their frightened, bone-white faces would allow.

CHAPTER 6

An Arrested Development

PRINCIPAL DOOLEY, standing on the wooden floor in front of the stage, handed Darren and Jamie their check. He complimented them on a terrific show and added, "I must admit you even had *me* fooled with those tricks. Can you tell me how you did them if I promise to keep it a secret?"

"Oh, you know us magicians," said Darren. "We never like to tell how it's done, heh, heh."

"Yeah, we wouldn't tell you even if we knew!" added Jamie, who picked up on a quick "Can it" look from Darren.

"Ah, always keep 'em guessing, huh?" chuckled the principal as he shook the boys' hands.

"We're sorry about the curtains," said Darren.

"Oh, no, you did us a favor," said the principal. "We've been trying to get the Board to replace those for years. Now they'll have to! Well, so long, guys, and keep up the good work!"

He left the auditorium, and the two, now alone, let loose

with cries of shock and amazement.

"Oh, my God!" shouted Darren.

"Wild, dude!" spewed Jamie. "That was crazy!"

"*Way* beyond my scope of understanding! And that wind again! Can you say 'super freaky?'"

"Yeah, I don't believe it," Jamie concurred. "All I said was, 'I wish I was a real magician,' and the doors blew open like they'd been hit by cannonballs!"

"Yeah! Whew! They just, they . . . Wait, what did you say?"

"The doors. They blew open like they'd been hit by—"

"No, I mean before that. About the wish."

"Oh, yeah. I said I wished I was a real magician and, uh, that's when the wind blew the . . ." Jamie stopped himself, and the boys looked at each other. "Do you think that wish had something to do with it?"

"I don't know," said Darren. They stood there, thinking. "Jamie . . ."

"Huh?"

"Do something."

"Like what?"

"I don't know. Try to make a bird appear."

"How? We didn't rehearse anything like that."

"Just say it. Say 'Bird appear.'"

Jamie shrugged. "Bird appear."

At once, the room echoed with the sound of chirping. Startled, they looked about. Out of nowhere, a multi-colored tropical parrot appeared in front of their faces and flew high above them. The boys' eyes looked ready to pop out of their heads as Maxwell barked and leaped about.

"That looks just like my Aunt Rosa's parrot!" exclaimed Jamie. "Prettiest thing I ever saw."

"Try telling it to disappear."

"Bird, disappear!" Jamie said, and the chirping ceased. The parrot was gone. Maxwell searched about in frustration.

Jamie, testing, tried again. "Birds appear!"

And suddenly, the room filled with hundreds of chirping birds of all varieties. Darren and Jamie shielded themselves to guard against the onslaught. Maxwell, whimpering, ducked under a stack of folded chairs.

"Make them disappear!" pleaded Darren.

"Birds, disappear!" Jamie ordered, and, in a wink, they vanished.

Darren turned and looked at Jamie like he was seeing a ghost. "You . . . you're a . . . you're a real magician!" he exclaimed.

"Yeah. Yeah, I am," said Jamie, not quite believing it himself.

"But how . . . ?"

Jamie thought for a moment and it dawned on him. "The guy! The guy in the thrift shop who said he was a genie from some galaxy! He told me to make some wishes!"

"That customer? No way, man, that guy was just a nutcase!"

"But wait, and that kid in the audience. . . . I said I wished that I was a real magician so that I could make him disappear, and suddenly, real magic was happening."

"Yeah, that's right, that's right. But . . . nah, it's just not possible. No one can . . . Hey, wait a minute. You wished something else, too."

"What?"

"Mosi. You wished that Mosi would win the lottery. You said that to him in his store."

"Yeah, yeah. I wished that he'd win the lottery so he'd get a new TV. That was right before, uh . . . the wind blew in."

Darren paused, realizing the truth. "And then he won the lottery."

"Yeah."

"Oh my God," said Darren. "We're so stupid! Why didn't we see this before? Do you know what this means, Jamie?"

"Yeah. I'm a freak. A mutant."

"What? No! Well, I mean, not *only* that. Jamie . . . we are going to be great magicians. We're going to be the greatest magicians in the world! We'll be able to do *anything!*"

"Yeah? Yeah! *Oh*, yeah!"

"How many wishes did that guy say you had?"

"I think it was three."

"Just like in all those old stories, huh? Well, you've got two down and one to go."

"You really think that's what happened?"

"It's the only explanation," said Darren. "But I always thought that genies came out of a bottle or something, and you're supposed to rub it first."

"Yeah, like a big puff of smoke and . . . Hey, wait a minute, there *was* a bottle."

"Where?"

"In the thrift shop. I was rubbing it to wipe off the dirt."

"And when did the guy start talking to you?"

Jamie thought carefully. "Right after that."

Darren looked at Jamie intently. "We've got to get that bottle."

"Why?"

"*Why?* The genie's in there! We can get more wishes! And if we're gonna be the greatest magicians, then we've gotta make sure that no one else can be, either!"

ONE OF THE TEACHER'S AIDES drove the boys back to Jamie's house, and they immediately ran to catch a bus to the thrift shop. The entrance was locked; the place had closed twenty minutes earlier. They peered through the glass door and windows that spanned half the block, but saw no signs of life.

"Oh, man, what are we gonna do?" said Darren, a bead of sweat rolling off his forehead. "We have to get that bottle!"

"Hey, wait," said Jamie brightly. He cleared his throat. "Genie bottle, appear in my hand!"

Nothing happened.

"No, no, remember?" said Darren. "The genie said you couldn't move the bottle with a wish. I guess that goes for your magic, too."

"Oh, right. We'll just have to wait till tomorrow."

"Tomorrow? Man, a lot could happen before tomorrow! We have to get that thing now!"

"But the place is closed."

"Yeah, yeah, but . . ." A scheme formed in Darren's head. Jamie sensed trouble brewing, as he always could when Darren got a certain glimmer in his eye.

"But what, Darren?"

"If I'm not mistaken, you're a real magician. You can get us in there."

"How?"

"Tell the door to open."

"No, no, we could get in trouble. That'd count as breaking in."

"What, talking to a door? That wouldn't even count as conversation."

"Yeah, but wait—wouldn't I be using up my last wish?"

"Not if you don't say 'I wish.' It's just, it's part of your magic powers. Now, try it."

"Well . . . all right. Here goes." Jamie stared at the door lock. "Open, store!"

Nothing happened. Darren said, "Well, that didn't—"

He stopped, hearing a low humming sound, which quickly grew louder. The boys exchanged worried glances as the entire store seemed to shake. Suddenly, the shop's entire glass facade, including both the door and the expanse of plate glass windows, shattered into bits with violent *cracking* and *crashing*. The boys cringed as they shielded their eyes to avoid the airborne shards of glass.

When the dust settled, they looked, mouth agape, at the destruction. Broken glass littered the sidewalk.

"You were supposed to say, open *door,* not open *store,*" said Darren, thrilled just the same at the outcome.

"Wicked!" was all Jamie could reply. They looked at each other, wondering what to do.

"Let's get the bottle!" said Darren.

"Yeah!"

They climbed in through the open window frames and hurried toward the costume area.

A HALF A MILE AWAY, Officers John Tierney and Margo Hellard were making their routine neighborhood rounds. Tierney was thirty-five, dark-haired, handsome and fit, with ten years on the force. The dirty-blond rookie officer, Hellard, was shorter than her fellow officers, but made up for it with her thick, strong physique and serious manner.

Their police car radio crackled out an urgent call. "Twenty-four, come in Twenty-four," squawked a dispatcher.

Tierney pressed an intercom button below the steering wheel. "Twenty-four to base. Tierney and Hellard here."

"We have a robbery in progress at the Salvation Army Thrift Shop on Sherman Avenue. A driver spotted two white males breaking and entering—apparently teenagers."

"We're on our way."

Tierney triggered the siren, spun a U-turn, and floored it.

"Proceed with extreme caution," the dispatcher continued.

"They're probably very dangerous."

"Are they armed?" asked Tierney.

"Don't know, but, well, they're robbing a thrift shop. They've got to be pretty hard up."

"Good point. Send backup. Over."

The police car wailed onto the main drag.

IN THE SEMI-DARKNESS of the store, Jamie spotted the yellow cardboard box beneath the same row of pants.

"Got it!" he said. He looked in the box and his face fell—old shoes took the place of the antiques. "It's not here!"

"Oh, no!"

"Someone must have bought it!"

"Maybe they just moved it," hoped Darren.

"Maybe. But it could be anywhere."

They looked about and began tearing through everything around them.

"Freeze and put your hands up!" Officers Tierney and Hellard pointed their guns directly at the boys. Jamie and Darren raised their arms with startled yelps.

"Drop to the floor!" barked Hellard. The boys fell to their stomachs.

"Please!" pleaded Jamie. "We were only looking for a bottle!"

"A bottle?" asked Tierney, cocking an eyebrow.

"Yes! I swear!"

"Oh, a wise guy, huh?" said Hellard. "How did you bust the

windows? Rocks? Bricks?" She looked about for evidence.

"Yeah, that was real bright, breaking *all* the windows," added Tierney. "A little overexcited were we?"

"Actually, we didn't break anything," said Darren. "I, I mean not really."

"Uh-huh. It happened by magic?" needled Tierney.

"Well, as long as you mention it," said Jamie, "that *is* sort of how it—"

"Shut up and put your hands behind your backs. You're under arrest," barked Hellard as she and Tierney whipped out handcuffs. The boys whimpered as the officers cuffed the two with dual cranks of the locks. Tierney took down their names and led them to the door.

"You have the right to remain silent," recited Hellard. "Anything you say can and will be held against you in a court of law . . ."

Once outside, Tierney and Hellard examined the demolished windows and shook their heads. Three police cars appeared at the end of the block, sirens blasting.

Darren had an idea. "Psst!"

"What?" whispered Jamie.

Darren drew his attention to the windows and hissed, "Magic."

"Magic? What magic?"

"Shut up, you two," snapped Hellard. "You'll have plenty of time for chit-chat down at the precinct."

Jamie looked at the windows. Seconds later, the squad cars

flew up to the curb. Six officers jumped out, followed by Police Chief Joe Belson, a tall, rugged, heavily built man whose strong, robust arms bulged from his crisp tan uniform.

"All right, what-a-we-got here?" he asked in a deep no-nonsense tone.

"Sir, these two suspects, uh, Darren Jackson and Jamie Jenks, broke into the store. We arrived on the scene and apprehended them," crowed Tierney.

"How did they get in?" the chief asked.

The officers were surprised by the question. Hellard said, "Well, they must have picked up some bricks and—" She and Tierney turned toward the store.

There wasn't one broken window.

"These windows!" exclaimed Tierney, aghast. "They were busted a moment ago!"

"Pardon me?" said Belson, clearly annoyed.

"The windows," continued Tierney. "They, uh . . . Well, they . . . It *seemed* that, uh, they were, uh . . . "

"They were broken, sir," confirmed Hellard, equally flabbergasted. "All of them."

Belson folded his arms and sighed. "They were . . . all broken," he repeated.

"Yes, sir," she said firmly. "And there was broken glass all down the sidewalk."

"She's right, sir," Tierney added, scratching his head. "They were completely destroyed as of . . . a moment ago."

Belson approached the windows and gave them a solid rap.

He turned and cleared his throat. "Care to tell me why they appear to be intact at this particular moment?"

"No, sir," said Tierney. A stony silence followed.

"Uh, he means we can't, sir," said Hellard. "We . . . We have no explanation for it."

"Uh-huh. Well. Suppose we ask these boys about this." Belson turned to the duo. "Did you gentlemen break these windows and then replace them while nobody was looking?" he asked with more than a hint of sarcasm. The boys shook their heads and shrugged. "Mm-hmm," continued Belson. "Did you break into the store?"

"No, sir," said Darren. "The door opened . . . by itself . . . so naturally we thought we could go in."

Belson checked the door as Tierney and Hellard watched in disbelief. It was open, with no sign of damage or tampering. Tierney gave his head a quick shake, hoping to clear his mind.

"Were the lights on when you entered?" asked Belson.

"No, sir," replied Darren. "We, uh, figured there was a blackout."

Belson gave him an incredulous glare. "A blackout. The door was open, there was nobody in the store, and you figured it was due to a blackout."

"Yes, sir," said Darren.

"I see. Tierney? Hellard?"

"Yes, sir?"

"You are each hereby given three weeks sick leave, effective immediately. Get some rest and, for God's sakes, get your heads together. We can't have officers of the law seeing things that aren't there."

They both wholeheartedly agreed. "Yes, sir. Thank you, sir."

Belson turned to another officer, a sturdy, sandy-haired man with a crisp gray moustache. "Jeffers, uncuff these kids and take them down to the station. There's something fishy here, though I'm not sure what."

"Yes, sir," said Jeffers.

Darren and Jamie gulped in unison. This was going to be trouble. Big trouble.

CHAPTER 7

Ainsley Grosspucker

A YOUNG NEWSPAPER PHOTOGRAPHER snapped photos of a Latino desk clerk working in the busy Washington Police Headquarters.

"Pretend I'm not here, Miss," he said. "I just need a few more shots."

"This'll be in tomorrow's paper?" asked the clerk.

"Yep. It's part of a front page report on how overworked this precinct is."

"Well, it's about time somebody noticed," said the clerk, and she spun a family photo around toward the camera. "Can you get my husband and kids in there?"

"No problem. Now just try to look, uh, exhausted." The woman leaned back and dabbed her forehead with a tissue. "Perfect," said the photographer, his camera shutter snapping furiously.

A few desks away, Darren and Jamie sat in front of Officer Jeffers, who filled out forms.

"Address?" he asked while looking down at the papers.

"Which one of us?" asked Darren.

"You," he said, not looking up.

"Umm . . . is that absolutely necessary?"

Now Jeffers glared at Darren. "What?"

"Well, it's just that my mom lives there, too, and I really don't want to drag her into this. She might, uh, be upset. You understand, don't you?" He chuckled charmingly.

"She'll only be dragged into this as much as she cares to be when I call her in a minute," sneered Jeffers. "Now, what is your address?"

"Well, okay, it's, uh, it's . . . We just moved, so I just gotta remember. Now, let's see . . ." Darren scratched his chin while giving Jamie a piercing, wide-eyed stare.

"Don't ask me, dude," Jamie whispered. "I didn't even know you moved."

"No, man," hissed Darren. "Do some—"

"Pardon me?" said Jeffers, growing plentifully annoyed. "Didn't quite catch that."

"I said I remembered now. Yes. It's Seven-one-seven, uh, Humbleton Court. That's here in D.C., uh . . . somewhere."

"Zip code?"

"Yes, the zip code we will now be using is, uh . . . I believe that it's—"

"What in the world?" said Jeffers. The form was suddenly blank. "I swear I just wrote that down. I hate these cheap pens." He tossed the pen into a wastebasket and grabbed another. "Okay, the address again."

"All right. That would be Seven-two-six—"

The new pen suddenly rose from Jeffer's hand. Shocked, he jerked back in his chair.

"What the heck? What is this?" he exclaimed.

"I'm a magician!" Jamie announced gleefully.

"A magician? You're making this happen?" asked Jeffers.

"Yeah! Watch this!"

The pen jumped higher, then soared down to the paper, where it quickly scribbled Jamie's name and address.

"How about that?" exclaimed Jamie. "Pretty good, huh?"

Darren was worried—Jamie's address on the form wasn't going to help their cause.

"Oh, my God!" said Jeffers. "Hey, Pennick! Gordon! Macy! Come over here and look at this!"

The officers sauntered over, along with other staffers. As they neared, their mouths dropped open, astounded by the self-propelled pen.

"Holy Toledo!" said one officer. The others added similar exclamations while the alert photographer hungrily snapped photos.

"This guy's a magician, and he's making it happen!" said Jeffers.

"What, are there strings?" asked a female detective, looking closely and squinting.

"Can't tell you," said Jamie playfully as Jeffers moved his hand around the pen. "It's just magic! Watch!" The pen cap leapt off the table and clicked onto the pen, which then sailed back into the pencil holder. "Ta-daaaaa!"

The group laughed and applauded, saying "Amazing!" and "Holy moly!"

"What else can you do?" asked a clerk, but Chief Belson burst through the crowd.

"What's going on here?" he bellowed. "All the work is finished? All the bad guys are behind bars?"

"Uh, sir, you really should see this," said Jeffers. "Quick, do another one. Here." He handed Jamie a wrapped candy from a dish. Jamie took the candy and cupped it in his hands.

"Well, uh, you shouldn't eat this because too much of it will give you . . . cavities!"

He opened his hands. In place of the candy was a pair of plastic clacking jaws with ugly brown and yellow teeth. Seeing that Belson was amazed, the others laughed and applauded once again.

"Well, I don't know how he did it," said Belson, "but this is a police station, not a circus. Everybody get back to work immediate—"

The teeth jumped from Jamie's hands and bounced around the desk, mimicking Belson: "This is a police station, not a circus! This is a police station, not a circus!"

Darren looked worriedly at Jamie, who, truth be known, was not yet in complete control of the effects. If he thought about something happening, it might very well come to pass.

It was now Belson's jaw that dropped as the teeth settled on the desk. "Well, I'll be a lamb's behind," he said. "Tell me how you did that!"

"Uh, I can't," said Jamie.

"Oh, you can't, huh? You're this close to lockup and you can't tell me how you did that?"

"Uh, well you see, Chief Belson, sir, magicians never reveal their secrets," explained Darren.

A deathly pause followed as everyone braced for the husky chief's usual blowup. Instead, he said, "Yeah, well, I always hated magicians." The group chuckled, relieved. "Remind me never to invite these guys over for poker night. We'd lose our shirts, wouldn't we?"

"Uh, yeah, you'd definitely lose your shirt," said Jamie, playing along. But suddenly, his words became another magical action—Belson's shirt started ripping right off of him.

"Heeeeeey!" shouted Belson, unable to control his runaway garment.

"Jamie!" yelled Darren, but Jamie was helpless to stop it. The chief's shirt tore to shreds and fell away. This also had the effect of loosening his belt, causing his pants to fall to his knees. The result was a startling sight—the chief stood before his staff, wearing a bright purple, pink, and blue "Barney the Dinosaur" tank top T-shirt, complete with matching purple polka-dotted boxer underpants. The shirt showed the smiling dinosaur dancing, with "I ♥ Barney" at the top in rounded letters and "Super-dee-duper!" at the bottom. The hairs of Belson's puffy chest bushed out over the low neckline, and his ample stomach spilled from the bottom. Everyone gasped and froze in amazement, realizing that their gruff, fearless boss wore Barney undergarments. Belson's face registered horror as he tried to cover up the evidence.

Darren glanced quizzically at Jamie as if to say, "Is the Barney stuff part of the magic?" Nope, Jamie suggested with a shake of his head—the chief had the garments on all along.

The photographer snapped a photo. He finally had a shot the likes of which no one else at the paper had ever taken—or seen.

"CHIEF BELSON UNDERCOVER" blazed the headline in the next morning's *Washington Post.* It was easily the most embarrassing story in the paper's one hundred and thirty-two year history. A large color photo showed the feared and revered police chief attempting to cover up his colorful underwear while surprised officers looked on. ("Yeah, okay, I like Barney," the chief sheepishly explained in the article. "He . . . He makes me feel safe.") A second, smaller shot showed Jamie and Darren displaying the rotten clacking teeth.

One copy of the paper was sitting on a desk in the office of Ainsley Grosspucker, a thin, wiry, forty-two-year-old local talent agent who, at the moment, was pleading with an older, balding client. The client, grasping a worn wooden suitcase, headed for the door.

"You can't leave!" begged Ainsley. "You're the only act I have left!"

"There's a good reason for that, Grosspucker! You're a swindler and a cheapskate, and that's putting it nicely!"

"I'll make up for it, I promise!"

"Forget it! Seven years with you, and what's it gotten me? A few lousy birthday parties, and you had the nerve to take most of what I made for them anyway, you petty thief!"

"But there's not much of a calling for ventriloquist acts anymore. You've got to take what you can get!"

"Oh, yeah?"

The man lifted his suitcase and a squeaky voice seemed to pipe from inside, "We'll get plenty of work elsewhere, you screwy little string bean!"

"Hey, that's terrific!" said Ainsley, sweat spilling from his brow. "You, you're better than I thought. Maybe I can book you at—"

Slam. The door was shut and the man was gone. Ainsley slowly sank into the shabby leather chair behind his desk.

"Maybe I can book you at my funeral," he uttered sadly.

He wasn't joking—Ainsley was a man at the end of his rope. He was done with scrounging out a meager living and having no social life to speak of. He racked his brain trying to figure out where he'd gone wrong. Sure, he could have been fairer, he thought. Sure, he could have been more honest. If only those were traits of the big time agents whose ranks he longed to join. *I was just doing whatever was needed to make it to the top*, he thought. Instead, he'd hit rock bottom. His big dreams were destroyed, and with it, his life. And if that wasn't bad enough, his wife, whom he loved and adored beyond all reason, had left him for . . . Well, that was too painful for him to even think about.

He opened a drawer and pulled out a pistol. Beneath it were two photographs, which he picked up and studied. The first was a black and white snapshot of his brother and himself as kids, posing in a living room with their smiling mother. A beaming Ainsley clutched a toy fire engine while his brother, as if singing, held out a top hat and a cane. The other was of his pretty blond ex-wife and himself on their wedding day—they had shoved cake into each other's faces and were laughing.

He observed the photos with great sorrow, then returned them to the drawer. Better to end it quickly, he determined. He laid his head face down on his desk, cocked his gun, and pointed it at the base of his skull. He scrunched his face as he drew up the nerve to finish the job.

But wait a second, he thought. Who would have to clean up the mess after they removed his body? That unpleasant task would likely fall upon kindly old Mrs. Scrutin, the building's half-blind assistant superintendent. Well, no matter if it ruined her day, he decided. He wouldn't be alive, so why care? But, well, she *had* been nice to him; he could at least make her job a little easier. He grabbed the morning paper and spread it out on his desk, knocking a dented coffee pot and empty soda cans onto the floor with a clatter.

Satisfied, he rested his head on the paper and lifted the gun to his skull once again. But something caught his eye. He sat up and looked at the photo of Chief Belson, and then at Darren and Jamie. The caption under their photo read "*A strange duo's strange magic.*" Ainsley's eyes lit up. Could it be true? Yes, there it was—a new act; hope for the future!

He snatched up the paper in his shaky, clammy hands and started reading. He was still holding the gun, however, and *bang*—it went off, shattering a ceramic pencil holder and sending his chair reeling backward onto the floor. All was silent.

"Ow," he uttered.

CHAPTER 8

The Mischievous Mimes

"I THINK IT'S TERRIBLE!" said Marie, wagging the news-paper in Jamie and Darren's faces in the kitchen. "My boy in the news for breaking into a store! And you too, Darren? I can't even believe it!"

"But Momma," said Jamie, "we just wanted to get some-thing there, and the door, uh, just opened."

"Yeah, when we . . . tried it," added Darren.

"The police let us go without filing any charges."

"Well, you're just lucky," insisted Marie. "They could just as easily have thrown you both into jail."

"But they decided we didn't do anything illegal," reasoned Jamie.

"Yeah, and we did some pretty amazing magic," said Darren.

"Magic!" echoed Marie, disgusted.

"That's right, Momma. You wouldn't believe what I can do now. You want to see something amazing?"

"Yes, your bed made and your room straightened by the time I get back from the store. I'll fall on my face, I'll be so amazed! Now, I will decide your punishment for this whole thing later. Goodbye!" She stormed out of the house, slamming the door behind her.

The two friends just stood there and sighed.

"What trick were you going to do for her?" asked Darren.

"I was going to clean my room by just saying, umm, clean yourself, room."

At once, they heard squeaking, rattling, and tossing coming from Jamie's room. The boys sprinted upstairs, peered in, and caught the last remaining items arranging themselves neatly on a shelf. The room was tidy and spotless.

"Wow!" said Jamie. "You want me to do your room, too? I can just say it, and it'll happen right from here."

"No, no," said Darren. "If my mother's standing there, she'll faint dead away. I'm already in enough trouble as it is."

"Oh, yeah, you, too. Dude, we gotta get famous fast, or for sure I'm gettin' grounded for a month at least."

"Well, becoming famous will be easy. We just gotta . . . We just gotta . . . uhhhh . . . " Darren's voice trailed off as he realized he hadn't the slightest idea how to proceed.

"We just need one of those, uh, agents, right?" said Jamie. "Famous people have agents that put them on TV and all."

"Yeah, that's it. But where do you find an agent in Washington, D.C.?"

Just then, the doorbell rang and the boys walked down and answered it. There, wearing an oversized brown jacket and a thin olive green tie, was a slim man with a drawn, pallid face. He had a crooked smile with teeth to match.

"Well, if it isn't the strange magic duo!" he said brightly.

Darren cocked an eyebrow. "And you would be . . ."

"Allow me to introduce myself. I'm Ainsley Grosspucker—Washington's premiere talent agent."

"A talent agent? Darren, it's a talent agent!"

"Named Grosspucker? Where'd you get a name like that?"

"I know it's unusual, but I guess you could say that I'm an unusual man. I like to make people into big stars. Anyone here up for that?"

"Darren, d'ja hear that? He's gonna make us into stars!"

"And how would you do that?" asked a skeptical Darren. He wanted nothing more than to believe the guy, but he figured that nothing good falls into anyone's lap *this* easily. There had to be a catch.

"Well, judging from what I read in the paper, you guys already know your stuff," said Ainsley, "so I plan to launch you right away with local TV shows, and we'll work our way up from there."

"TV, Darren! He's gonna put us on the tube!"

Darren felt distrustful of him, though he wasn't sure why. Something about him just seemed a little . . . wormy. "Uh-huh," he said slowly. "And what do you get out of it?"

"Why, a portion of what you make, of course. You just have to sign a contract that pays me a percentage of your salary, and we're on our way."

"Where do we sign?" asked Jamie eagerly.

"Uh, just a minute," said Darren. "What kind of percentage are we talking about here?"

"Oh, it's a usual ten percent deal. Why don't we give it a try?"

Jamie looked at Darren like a hungry poodle awaiting a biscuit.

"Well, we've got to ask for our mothers' permissions first," said Darren.

"Well, sure," said Ainsley, "but if they say no, you're going to miss the opportunity of a lifetime. Are you sure you want to take that chance?"

"We're teenagers, Darren," declared Jamie. "We're old enough to make our own decisions from here on in!"

Darren thought further. "You know what?" he said finally. "You're right. Sometimes you just gotta go for it. Let's do it, let's sign that thing."

"Brother-man, yes!" exclaimed Jamie. "Now that's what I'm talking about!"

"Great!" said Ainsley, whipping a contract out of his pocket. "Boys, I promise you we're onto big things together, and quickly. You are going to be one of the top teams in magic, and I'm going to get you there."

"Bring it on!" yelled Jamie.

TRUE TO HIS WORD, Ainsley didn't waste time. The following week, the team was booked on *Wake Up, Washington*, a local morning talk show starring the broad-shouldered, square-jawed Tad Le Vine. Tad was a slick, smug, arrogant host who was often rude to his guests. He once sent a young film actress crying off the set when he revealed, on the air, that she was really ten years older than she claimed to be and that she only got cast in her movies because her father was a big Hollywood director. "Sure, go on, get out of here!" he chided as the actress fled the studio in tears. "Your movie's going down the tubes anyway and so's your career!"

The show's producers immediately received thousands of letters and e-mails demanding that Tad be fired, but his contract stated that he would be paid a million dollars if that were to happen. The producers simply couldn't afford to get rid of him. The show's talent department found it hard to book important guests after that, so they had to be inventive with their selections. Jamie and Darren's picture in the paper (along with the Barney-clad Chief Belson) was all Ainsley needed to get the boys on the show.

Moments before their appearance, the two were in their dressing room, teeming with nervous excitement.

"How do I look?" asked Jamie, straightening his sharp purple sports jacket.

"Most magnificent, man!" said Darren, tugging the sleeve of his matching outfit. "Okay, remember, first we make the dog appear, and then—"

The stage manager stuck his head in the door. "We're ready for you, guys."

"Here it goes!" said Darren.

"Hey," said Jamie, stopping in his tracks. "Let's do it for Mosi."

"Yeah," agreed Darren. "This one's for good ol' Mosi!"

They did an overhead hand slap, yelled "Deeeal!" and ran out of the room.

Unfortunately for the boys, Tad Le Vine was in one of his notorious foul moods, which he seldom hid on camera. Reading a cue card, he said, "My next guests are two of Washington's own homebred talents—two teenage magicians who will astound you with their amazing feats." He then added, "Oh, yeah, I can't wait to see this, huh? I'm not a big fan of magicians, personally—they're just there to try to fool you. I mean, how is *that* entertaining? And most of them do tricks that anyone with half a brain could do." He laughed smugly.

"*What?*" said an astonished Darren, staring at a TV monitor backstage. Jamie emitted a screech of disdain.

"I mean, come on," continued Tad. "They're really just half a step above *mimes*. You've seen mimes, right? Those white-faced goons who pretend that everything's invisible? Don't you just hate them?" He spoke in a childish, pinched voice. "Oh, look, I'm building a cage around me and it's getting smaller! Oh, look, I'm walking into the wind and I can't move!" Back to his normal voice: "Yeah, great. Hey, mimes, get a real job and give me a freakin' break, ya no-talent losers! Anyway, I'm told that these guys might be able to do some half-interesting *magic,* but we'll be the judges of that, won't we?"

Darren, angry with the sour host, had an idea, which he whispered to Jamie. Jamie nodded, closed his eyes, and murmured to himself.

"Okay, so here they are," announced Tad. "Darren Jackson and Jamie Jenks, otherwise known as—well, isn't *this* clever—Jackson and Jenks."

The studio audience applauded and the duo strode out. With a dash of instant magic, they now wore mime outfits, complete with red and white striped shirts, black leotards, French berets, and white gloves. White makeup covered their faces, along with black and red outlines of their mouths and eyes. The boys ignored Tad's look of surprise as they settled into gray cloth chairs next to his desk.

"Wait a minute, I thought you guys were magicians," said Tad.

"We are! We're magical mimes!" explained Jamie.

"I see, and what does that mean exactly?" asked Tad, giving the audience a devilish wink.

"We'd like to show you," said Darren. He and Jamie walked to the front of Tad's desk. "Could you come help us, please?"

"Well, okay, why not?" said the host, laughing a bit nervously. He walked between the two. "All right, let's see some, uh, magic, mime-boys. Whataya got for us?"

The duo pretended to build a cage completely around Tad. They moved their hands quickly about, making it appear as if they were touching a surface.

"What's this?" mocked Tad, reprising his childish voice. "Oh, they're building an invisible cage around meeee. Oooh, I'm scaaared, aren't you? Oooh, look, I'm in a cage, I'm in a cage!" He laughed at the boys, who continued working diligently. "Are we done? Am I stuck in a *magic caaaage?*"

"Yeah, that's it," said Darren, and he and Jamie walked calmly back to their seats.

"Well, if that's the best you can do, I thank you for being on the show, and . . ." Something stopped Tad when he tried to move—something he couldn't see. "What the . . . ?" He tried walking again, but he banged into an invisible barrier. "Well, heh, heh, that's just, uh . . ." He shook his head in disbelief and took a step in the opposite direction. "Oof!" he blurted as he again slammed into an unseen force. His confusion turned to panic when he reached out and touched a solid, invisible wall. He gasped and tried pushing against it, but his attempt was futile—he was firmly sealed inside a magical cage. The audience laughed as he struggled to escape.

"Oh, my God, I'm really trapped inside here!" cried Tad, wriggling and writhing about. "Let me out of here! Let me ooooout!" He felt the cage beginning to close in around him. *"It's getting smaller!"* he shrieked. *"It's going to kill me! Do something! Heeeeeeeeeelllp!"*

"You can help yourself," offered Darren calmly.

"How?"

"Pretend to build a door."

"What?"

"Build a door," Darren repeated.

"Better hurry, dude" said Jamie. "That thing's gettin' mighty small."

The cage walls now seemed to press against Tad's shoulders, and he screamed. With no other choice, he pretended to build a door, making an outline with his hands.

"Okay!" he yelled.

"Now open it and walk out," said Darren.

Tad turned an invisible knob. The unseen door opened and he spilled out of the cage, tripping onto the shiny black floor. He stumbled to his feet and took deep, reassuring breaths as the very amused studio audience applauded.

Darren whispered to Jamie, who nodded and again muttered a few words. Suddenly, a gust of wind hit Tad hard, but nothing and no one else was affected. The gust knocked him back against the invisible cage as the audience laughed anew.

"Aaaah, heeeeeeeeeelp! I can't move!" he yelled. "How do I get out of *this?"* The wind's force blew his hair wildly and made his cheeks ripple.

"You have to build a wall in front of you to block the wind!" shouted Darren. "Make it with your hands!"

Tad quickly mimed building a wall in front of himself, which was difficult due to the tornado-force flurry storming against him. The moment he finished, the wind ceased. The audience applauded wildly as Tad, winded and unstable, turned to the boys. He clenched his fists and squinted fiercely, his face turning bright red.

"I'm going to kill you!" he roared, and he lurched toward them. He ran smack into his still-standing invisible wall and fell, landing flat on his back. He yelled, then quickly got up and raced at them once more—and again banged into the wall and fell. He grew more manic, repeatedly trying to attack the boys, even as his audience was teary with laughter. His yelling sounded more and more inhuman, like the barking of an angry, rabid dog. Jamie and Darren looked at each other and smiled, very satisfied with how their first TV appearance was going.

Watching from offstage, Ainsley Grosspucker shook his head in wonder and delight—he was just as amazed as everyone. These guys were his ticket to the big time, he thought. He was sure of it. The only question in his mind was how to get these incredible boys on a *major* television program. It was almost impossible to get unknown magicians booked on a national network talk show no matter how good they were.

An unexpected event helped make this goal possible. Tad Le Vine provided the needed publicity for the act by actually losing his mind. As he continued to bang into the invisible wall, the show broke for a commercial break. Tad then bolted forward, yelling incoherently, his arms flailing about. He sprinted up through the audience and past the ushers, who were startled by his crazed, terrified glare. He continued into the lobby and out onto the street.

When the show returned from the break, it was without a host. Jamie, saving the day, jumped behind the desk and took over in his own goofy way. Darren joined in, and the show's producer, seeing the audience enjoying their antics, let them finish the hour. Jamie performed magic with items on the desk, turning each into a wide array of animals and objects.

When studio security guards finally caught up with Tad on the street a quarter of a mile away, they tried to calm him, but he kicked and screamed and spoke nonsensically: "The, it, wall, gone, knock, squish, and my nose hit on the . . . Witches! Warlocks! Witches! *Warlooooocks!*"

The security guards, holding him steady, sadly shook their heads. "Looks like we're back to lobby duty," said one of them. "This blowhard's show is certainly a goner."

CHAPTER 9

Fame, Fortune, and
the Amazing Ozlo

THE NEXT DAY, the lead story of every entertainment news show on TV told of how the notorious host Tad Le Vine was carted off to a mental hospital in a straightjacket after meeting up with the "extraordinary magical team of Jackson and Jenks." It wasn't long before Ainsley's phone was ringing off the hook with bookings for the boys (who, with their newly proud mothers' permissions, quickly left their old jobs).

The first show Ainsley chose was *Rise and Shine, USA, With Loomis Perkins and Kathryn Chase.* The hosting duo, a jovial, witty older man and his cute, perky young partner had the highest rated morning show in America. Ainsley thought it was perfect for the boys, and he flew them out to Hollywood for their national debut.

Backstage at the TV studio, hair and makeup people fussed over Darren and Jamie, who sat watching the show on a monitor. The attractive hosts were busily complimenting each other.

"You look amazing today, Kathryn. Have you done something new to your hair?"

"Oh, just brushed it, finally," she joked, to the audience's amusement. "That, and I had it done by my *fabulous* hairdresser, Paulo, at Arami's in West Hollywood. How about a hand for Paulo?" The audience complied with cheering and applause. "You look really good, too, Loomis," she continued. "Have you been working out lately?"

"What do *you* think?" he said, pulling back his sleeve and flexing his bicep.

She gave it a playful squeeze. "Yikes, you *have* been working out!"

"Well, the wife got tired of the gut, and you know *her*—she lets me know about it, so I started working with an amazing new trainer, Tony Garson. He's a terrific guy with a *great* personality. He and his entire staff over at Mako's Gym in Brentwood are really top notch."

Darren thought they seemed phony, just plugging the names of people they hired, probably to receive free services in return. He shook his head.

A bubbly Ainsley barged into the makeup room. "All right, guys, this is going to be great! You'll be big stars after this, and I mean bigger than The Amazing Ozlo!"

"I don't know, Ainsley," said Jamie. "He's the biggest ever, that guy."

"He'll be nothing by the time you two are through. By

the way, what tricks are you doing today? The producer said you didn't need to set up anything."

Darren looked at Jamie, who gave a shrug. Darren said, "We haven't the slightest idea what we're going to do."

Ainsley panicked. "But this is national television! You haven't even thought about what you're going to do when . . ." A smile leaked across his lips. "Oh, you guys can't put that one over on me! Okay, you can surprise me, too. I'll be out there sitting with your mothers. Break a leg, okay?"

"Thanks, Ainsley," they said. Ainsley gave them a goofy thumbs-up and made his way to the door.

"Hey, Ainsley," continued Darren, approaching him. "Hey, uh, I just really want to thank you for what you're doing. I didn't trust you at first, to tell you the truth, but, well, you're really coming through for us. Thanks a lot."

"Yeah, thanks, man," added Jamie, trailing Darren. "You're really kickin' it." The two gave him shoulder-to-shoulder hugs, slapping him on the back.

Ainsley was blown away. He was more used to being cursed at than being thanked, much less hugged. Plus, he had a terrible secret that he was feeling mighty guilty about.

"Uh . . . sure, guys," he said, nervously straightening his thin, olive-green tie. "Just doing my job. Well, see you after the show."

"Later, man," the boys chimed, and Ainsley exited.

"So what tricks *are* we going to do?" Darren asked Jamie.

"I don't know. Let's think."

They looked back up at the monitor. The hosts were still in

full mutual admiration mode, with Loomis taking the lead.

"And that song you wrote, Kathryn—'We're in This To-gether Together'—What a hit, and to hear you sing it at the People's Choice Awards, well, it was simply breathtaking. She was amazing, wasn't she, folks? Was Kathryn amazing or what?" The audience cheered and applauded.

"Thanks, everybody. Thanks, Loomis," she responded, preening. "Of course, it wouldn't have felt right if you hadn't been there, hosting. You are just, like, the best host that ever lived! Wasn't he *stupendous?*" The audience gave a repeat applause performance. "Our sponsor, Peppity Pop, must be really proud of you!"

"Oh, yeah," replied Loomis. "We love everyone over there at Peppity Pop. Greatest energy drink in the world, I kid you not. Thanks, Peppity Pop, we owe you one."

"Man, these guys are so phony!" said Darren. "How can they say all those things without gagging?"

"Maybe they mean it," suggested Jamie.

"Yeah, well, maybe they don't."

After a moment, Darren and Jamie looked at each other, having sparked precisely the same idea at precisely the same time. They were then escorted to a spot behind a screen for their entrance.

"Our next guests are either the greatest magicians in the world, or the greatest hypnotists," said Loomis. "Take a look at their appearance on *Wake Up, Washington,* with host Tad Le Vine."

The audience laughed uproariously as they viewed a clip of Tad continually falling down upon hitting the invisible wall.

"The episode put Le Vine in a mental hospital," continued Loomis, "and for those of us who know him, we can only say, Tad, make yourself at home." The audience tittered. "Now, please welcome the magical team of Jackson and Jenks!"

The crowd clapped as the boys entered with confidence and enthusiasm. They sat on stools with the hosts, who welcomed them and asked how they got their start. Darren told a story (the two had made up that morning) about learning from the great magicians and practicing for years. Jamie then launched into a few tricks from his seat, making birds and rabbits appear from nowhere. He uttered a few magic words, and Darren floated three feet above his stool. The audience applauded wildly.

Among them, clapping the loudest, were the boys' mothers, who sat together. Darren's mother, Regina Jackson, looked like an older, female version of Darren. She was overweight, with a flowery green dress and dark curly hair. Her eyes disappeared in a squint when she smiled, and smile she did. She and Marie were ecstatic that their sons were on their favorite morning show.

Jamie made a small silver ball appear and announced that it was his magic truth-telling orb. "Whoever touches this will have to tell the truth for five minutes," he explained.

Loomis and Kathryn had a good laugh as they felt the ball.

Jamie reiterated, "Whatever you say now will be the truth."

Loomis was the first. "Hmm, if I were to tell the truth, I doubt the show would be on tomorrow."

"Oh, no? And why is that, Loomis?" asked Kathryn.

"Because I would say how I'm really tired of this boring job. I really just want to relax at my enormous estate and order the servants around for the rest of my life."

"Oh, really. This is a tough gig for you, huh?" she chuckled. "I make eight million dollars a year, and all I have to do is look as gorgeous as I do anyway, and act interested in our guests."

"*Act* interested?"

"Of course. You don't think I really care one bit about the people who come here to plug their dumb TV shows and movies, do you? Please! I wouldn't watch one *second* of this show if I wasn't on it. What an enormous waste of time!"

The audience murmured, surprised by Kathryn's candor. Loomis was aghast.

"Waste of time? You're lucky to have this job at all, you overpaid, brainless ditz! If you hadn't dated the producer's son, they'd never have given you a second look!" The audience emitted a collective gasp.

"*What?* I had to put off a big touring career for your waste-dump of a show! I only took it so I could sell more CDs!"

"You mean that garbage that you pretend you wrote yourself? You really have no talent whatsoever! Your voice sounds like a test of the Emergency Broadcast System! It's a wonder *anyone* buys those bubblegum pop knockoffs with *thee* dumbest titles in the world!"

"Oh, really? How's *this* for a knockoff?" Kathryn reached over and ripped Loomis' toupee off his head. The audience "Ooooooohed" their surprise as she tossed it away. "You thought it was his own hair, huh? Guess again, losers! And don't you have anything better to do than to watch this meaningless tripe? *Get a life, people—please!"*

The audience gasped and started booing. Loomis was seeing red.

"Come here, you stupid twit!" he growled. He grabbed her hair and pulled. She bit his arm, but it was no use—he yanked off a fistful of blond extensions, leaving clumps of curly strands. "You thought that was all hers?" he roared. "Forget about it! And you should see all her acne in the morning! Her skin looks like the inside of a pomegranate!"

"Oh, yeah?" she countered. "It takes a team of surgeons to keep *your* face from falling off completely!"

The audience sat in shock as the hosts physically attacked each other—yelling, hitting, and grabbing clothes, hair, ears, and noses.

Darren and Jamie exchanged a look, and Jamie made the ball disappear.

THE FOLLOWING NIGHT, the boys sat in an ice cream parlor, downing triple banana splits. Jamie said he felt bad about exposing the hosts like that, but Darren told him he was being silly.

"We only got them to tell the truth," he reasoned, wiping

chocolate syrup off his chin. "We had nothing to do with their fight and them getting canned from the show and all."

Jamie agreed, but Darren secretly felt a little bad about it, too.

THINGS HAPPENED quickly from that moment on. The two were instantly the hot new showbiz sensation, and Ainsley was in heaven, his business booming. He had finally become the agent he'd always wanted to be, with three secretaries in his office fielding phone calls from the media. In one hour alone, he was contacted by five teen magazines as well as *People, Us, Time, Newsweek,* and *USA Today.* Gift baskets poured in from every TV talk show, each vying to have "Jackson and Jenks" on their program. They all wanted the chance to announce, "Tune in and see what the teenage wonders conjure up this time!"

The boys couldn't believe their luck as they flew around the country for live appearances, photo shoots, and interviews. They were on the local talk and news shows in every major city, demonstrating never-before-seen illusions, which they usually came up with right before each performance, if not on the spot.

In just one month from the day Jamie discovered the genie bottle, they were asked to star in their own TV special on NBC. The network, hoping for a summer ratings boost, wanted the show on as soon as possible, and the boys were happy to comply. Only three weeks later, *Jackson & Jenks,*

Master Magicians would beam into living rooms across the U.S., not to mention the forty-five other countries that signed on to carry the show. The eyes of the world were on the team, anxious to see what they would dream up for their big moment in the spotlight. This time, the boys were not leaving anything to chance—they had the show planned out from top to bottom.

On the big night, the two were onstage behind a shimmering silver curtain. They stood ready and waiting on a platform atop a giant golden staircase. Darren, wearing a snappy maroon tuxedo, identical to Jamie's, turned to his old friend.

"Are you ready, pal?"

"Ready, pal!"

"For Mosi?"

"For Mosi!"

A booming drum roll signaled the start of the show. The boys looked at each other and broke out in joyful yelps; they couldn't believe they were about to appear on their own national TV special. A stage manager whispered, "Guys, we're starting!" The two regained their composure, clearing their throats and straightening their outfits.

The director of the show sat in a control booth behind switchboards and TV monitors. "Go!" he ordered, and an army of colored lights hit the front curtain.

An announcer's voice boomed, "Ladies and gentlemen, *live* from the Kennedy Center in Washington, D.C., it's Jackson and Jenks, Master Magicians! Please note that the entire show will be performed for you just as the studio audience is see-ing it here for the first time. No camera tricks or editing of any kind will be used. Now, hold onto your hats, and please welcome the amazing magical team of Jackson and Jenks!"

Live rock music blasted as the curtain rose, and the boys walked down the staircase, beaming. *Jackson & Jenks* was spelled out in dazzling neon above the stairs, surrounded by hundreds of blinking lights. The pumped-up studio audience thundered their applause.

The boys' excited mothers sat in front, off to the side. Ten rows back, the rude freckle-faced boy from Darren's old job sat with his parents. "I know Darren!" he yelled. "He's my best friend from Jimmy Giraffe's!" His freckle-faced parents smiled while clapping.

The duo waved to the crowd and began the show. Two assistants wheeled out a long, thin, blue and silver box. Jamie climbed inside—his head protruded from one end and his feet from the other. A huge roaring, swirling circular blade was lowered from overhead, and the audience gasped as Darren guided it toward the center of the box. He made comical mean faces while the blade appeared to cut right through Jamie's middle with gruesome grinding and flying sawdust. Jamie, however, giggled as Darren inserted solid steel blades down the center of the box. He and the assistants then separated the box in two, showing that Jamie was cut in half.

The audience applauded, but the best was yet to come. Darren flipped open a door on the side of the box containing

Jamie's head and torso. Jamie stuck out his arm and clicked his fingers to bouncy jazz music. Darren then opened a lid on the box containing Jamie's legs. He clapped his hands, and Jamie's legs, attached to the bottom of his waist, leapt to the stage and broke into a spirited dance. The astonished audience clapped, cheered, and whistled their approval. Jamie's head swayed back and forth while his disembodied legs performed wild tap and jazz dance moves. Darren joined in the fun, and Jamie's legs danced next to him, perfectly matching his every step.

In the TV control booth, the director called out camera shots, then stopped and watched the monitors, mouth agape. "Well, I'll be darned," he said quietly. "They didn't do that in rehearsal." Then, remembering his job, he said, "Oh, camera four—go!"

THE DIRECTOR wasn't the only one who couldn't believe his eyes. Although tens of millions of people were enthralled by the show at that moment, none were studying it as closely as one particular man in an enormous mansion in Beverly Hills, California. The flat screen television he and his girlfriend were watching spanned almost an entire wall in one of the most flashy, expensive bedrooms that anyone had ever slept in. Most of the decor was done up in maroon, burnt orange, purple, black, and gold. In fact, much of it, like the garish canopied bed frame, was made of real gold. Dramatic lighting accentuated the ornate furniture, much of which was draped with flowing Indian silks and leopard skins. A roaring fire blazed in a sculpted opal fireplace next to a sunken, gem-lined Jacuzzi. The couple was seated on a plush purple sofa in front of a giant framed poster, which featured the two of them in a stage show of their own. It was the bedroom of The Amazing Ozlo, and The Amazing Ozlo was not happy. He sat forward in his blue silk Chinese bathrobe and squinted at the TV.

"They can't be doing this live!" he snarled, wiping the black flow of hair out of his face. "There's no way that this is live!"

"Honey, just relaaaaaax," cooed his girlfriend, Nadine. She was the beautiful, shapely blond assistant whom Jamie and Darren had seen on TV.

"How can I relax when those two clowns are, are *lying* to the entire world? They said it's happening live, but it's not even possible! I mean look at that!"

"Don't get yourself so worked up over it, sweetheart. Come here, come to Pooky Bear." She lay down behind him and wrapped an arm around his stomach. He brusquely knocked it away.

"Cut it out," he snipped. "They've got to be exposed. Everyone thinks they're so great, but they're nothing but a couple of wimpy kids with a special-effects computer program. The entire audience must be paid to act amazed while they're watching nothing but a blank screen!"

"Maybe, but don't get so upset about it, my kissy-face-honey-bunny. Everyone knows you're still the greatest ever."

"Well, of course that's true, but all everyone is talking about are these two bozos! They're complete amateurs!"

Nadine turned her attention to the show. Jamie's disembodied legs performed grand leaps about the stage.

"Well . . . you do have to admit they *are* pretty good," she said. Ozlo shot her a dagger-filled look. She proceeded with caution. "Or, I mean, umm . . . interesting. You know, for such . . . inexperienced beginners."

She looked back at the TV—Jamie's legs did a double flip in the air and returned to the box with a perfect landing. Darren shut the lid, and he and the assistants pushed the two boxes back together.

"Of course," added Nadine, "I've never actually seen anything like that before."

"Of *course* you've never seen anything like that before, don't you see? It's not really happening—it's all camera tricks!"

"But they said it was real. They can't lie on network television, can they?"

"All right, get out of here."

"What?"

"Get out and go away! And get your clothes and garbage out of here, too! You make me sick!"

"Honey, I was just—"

"Get out of here right now!"

Nadine, frightened by Ozlo's outburst, grabbed her purse. "But what about what you said last night?"

"What did I say?"

"You said you wanted to marry me, and—"

"Yeah, you wish! Now get out before I *throw* you out!"

Nadine made a beeline for the exit. She opened the door and turned back to him, yelling through tears. "You're just scared that those boys are better than you! Well, you know what? They are! They're a lot, lot better than you'll ever be, so just get used to it!"

Ozlo grabbed a china leopard head from a side table and hurled it near Nadine. She quickly slammed the door behind her, and *smash*—the statuette burst into bits against the wall. Ozlo let out a feral roar and toppled a side table. A lamp and two other statuettes *crashed* on the black marble floor.

The seething magician turned back to the show and watched as Jamie, restored and happy, popped out of the box. The audience leapt to its feet, cheering and applauding, while Ozlo's rage ebbed to a state of frustrated bewilderment.

"Where do they get those marvelous tricks?" he wondered aloud, laying waste to his theory of special effects.

There was a knock on the door.

"What?" he barked.

"It's Wilson."

"Yeah, come in."

Lance Wilson, Ozlo's loyal, trusted bodyguard, entered the room. He looked menacing; a bone-chilling figure to behold. The crater-deep scar that ran from the top of his left cheek to the edge of his mouth was almost lost among the scores of other lines wedged into his leathery, weather-beaten face. His comatose eyes, framed beneath his dark, protruding eyebrows, had a frozen glower that made men and women nervous and caused children and dogs to scurry away in fear.

"Everything okay, boss?" he asked. He had heard the commotion in the room, followed by Nadine storming past him and out the front door.

"Does everything *seem* okay? Come look at this."

Wilson watched the show. Darren talked to the audience while Jamie floated up and down behind him. Whenever Darren would look at him, Jamie would be on the ground. When he turned away, Jamie would float back up, mocking the supposedly clueless Darren. The audience was eating it up.

"How do you think they're doing that?" asked Ozlo.

"Wires?" guessed Wilson.

"Mm-hmm. Do you see any wires there?"

Wilson squinted at the screen. "No. I don't see any."

"Neither do I, Wilson. And there's an audience sitting right in front of them."

"So, uh . . . how are they doing it?"

"Just between you and me, Wilson?"

"Yeah."

"I haven't the slightest idea."

Wilson was surprised to hear this. Ozlo was the best in the world, he thought—at least that's what Ozlo always said.

"And do you know something, Wilson? That bothers me. That bothers me a lot. I'd really like to know how they do that. I really would."

Wilson thought for a moment. "Why don't you ask them?" he said.

Ozlo slowly turned to Wilson and spoke condescendingly. "I cannot *ask* them. It might make them think they were better than me. And they are not better than me . . . are they, Wilson?"

Wilson looked back at the TV. Jamie stood on a chair and Darren held a cloth in front of him. When he yanked it aside, Jamie had become a jumping toy poodle. Wilson stood there, utterly amazed.

"Wilson . . ."

"Oh, uh, they're nothing special. You're still the greatest, Ozlo. The best there ever was."

"Yes. Very good, very perceptive. And I do plan to remain the greatest. So . . . I need your help. And it involves a flight to Washington, D.C., in my private jet. Tonight."

Wilson turned to him, gleefully anticipating a crooked scheme. Wilson liked schemes—the dirtier, the better. And this was to be unlike any he'd ever been involved in before.

CHAPTER 10

When Glasses Fly

"IT'S THE BIGGEST HOUSE I've ever seen!" exclaimed Marie, her voice echoing throughout the three-story atrium. "Are you sure you and Darren can afford all this?"

"It's no problem, Mama," said Jamie, beaming. "Ainsley just bought it with the money we made. He said we needed it so we'd look good for the media and all."

Marie didn't respond, lost in wonderment at the enormous mansion she'd just stepped into. She didn't even know there were houses this large in Washington, other than the White House. It had eight bedrooms, a game room, a library, and a huge pool. The kitchen alone seemed bigger than most of the entire ground floors in all the houses she'd lived in.

"It's like a castle!" she gasped.

"Yeah, can you imagine the parties we can have here?" said Jamie, grinning.

"Now, Jamie," scolded Marie, "don't get carried away. Just because you bought a house doesn't mean you can just go do anything you please without asking my permission. You're still fifteen, and you can only visit here in the daytime until Darren's mother and I move in with you next month."

"Aw, Mom!"

"Don't you 'Aw, Mom' me, young man. I can ground you just like I did before."

"Sheesh! You mean being rich and famous doesn't even keep you from being grounded? What's the point?"

The library doors swung open, and Darren walked out in mid-argument with their housekeeper, Inga. Inga, twenty-four, was a thin, blue-eyed blonde with a thick Swedish accent.

"Inga," said an exasperated Darren, clutching an armful of blue towels. "The towels go in the towel closet, not in the library."

"Dat's vare *you* mide poot zem," challenged Inga. "*I* poot zem in ze library. Dat's vare *I* zay day go."

"Uh, Darren," said Jamie. "Look who's—"

"Yeah, but you see, Inga," continued Darren, speaking in a tone he had only used with his youngest Jimmy Giraffe customers. "The name of the place an item goes often has the name of the item in it. See, like . . . *towels* go in thee . . . *towel* closet. Get it?"

"Oh, yass, I ged eet. Zen I zuppose I'll jost go poot your *toys* in ze *toilet!*" She stormed up the grand staircase behind them while Darren just shook his head.

"Darren!" said Jamie.

He finally noticed Marie. "Oh, I'm sorry! Hello, Mrs.

Jenks. How do you like our little getaway here?"

"Little getaway?" replied Marie. "It's like four houses put together!"

"What, this creaky ol' crib?" said Darren, and they chuckled.

"Uh, but now boys, where did this *Inga* come from?" asked Marie.

"Oh, Ainsley sent her to help us run the place," explained Darren. "He said she used to do some sort of dancing act, you know, once upon a time."

"Yes, I'm sure she did," said Marie, pursing her lips. "You know, I don't think it's a very good idea to have someone like that running around here with—"

"Oh, my God, look at the time, Mama!" said Jamie, deftly switching gears. "We're on TV tomorrow and we haven't even begun to rehearse!"

"Another show so soon?" exclaimed Marie. "What are you going to be on tomorrow?"

"Uh, don't know exactly," said Jamie. "Ainsley didn't tell us yet."

"Well, you'd better get to work on it!" said Marie. "Where are all your tricks?"

Darren thought fast. "Oh, well, the carpenters are in the basement, uh, building them right now," he said, giving Jamie a stare, which, by now, Jamie understood to mean that he was to perform some magic. He muttered to himself, and sounds of sawing and hammering were heard beneath them.

"Oh! How exciting! I can't wait to see!" said Marie, heading to the front door. "I'm just so proud of both of you."

"Thank you," they replied.

Marie gave Jamie a kiss. "Now, I'll expect you back after you rehearse, Jamie. Remember what I said about staying here."

"Okay, Mama. Bye now!"

She left, and Jamie waved his hand—the sawing and hammering sounds ceased.

"Man, we almost had to get rid of Inga," Jamie said with a sigh of relief. "She's hot!"

"Yeah, but I wouldn't exactly call her the smartest fish in the sea," said Darren, strolling into the open, regal-looking game room. A pool table, with a racked set of balls, lay in wait.

"Nah, housekeeping's just new to her—she'll get the hang of it," said Jamie, who followed him in and grabbed a pool cue off the wall. "Hey, when do I get to tell my mom about the genie and all?"

"Never, man!" snapped Darren.

"Never? Why not?"

"Because she might tell someone and *they* might blow the whole thing."

"Yeah, maybe."

"Listen, Jamie," said Darren, carefully removing the silver rack from the pool balls, "we can't tell *anybody* about this *ever*. It has to stay between you and me. Promise?"

"I promise."

Darren chalked up his cue stick, grabbed the cue ball, and set up the first shot. "And don't forget," he said. "We've still got one more wish to go."

"I know. What do you think it should be?"

"I don't know. But I have a feeling it's going to be the biggest one yet." He hit the ball—it smacked into the formation and sent the balls reeling.

Darren thought that maybe the last wish would be to turn *him* into a magician, too. He was secretly jealous of Jamie having all the power, but it worked for now and he didn't want to waste what could be the final wish of their lifetimes.

Outside, Marie revved her car in the winding cobblestone driveway and gazed up at the mansion. It was a white palatial estate, surrounded by a stylish metal gate and beautiful lush trees and plants. On the front landing, a pair of twenty-foot Corinthian columns stood guard before the majestic entrance. Marie shook her head in wonder and smiled as she steered toward the gate, which slowly drew open for her.

She drove off, passing a plain brown sedan parked across the street. The sedan deftly pulled into the driveway as the gate was closing. The car door opened—the sinister-looking Lance Wilson stepped out and looked around, a black attaché case clutched in his hand. He attached a circular cloth insignia, with a picture of a magician fanning a deck of cards, to the front pocket of his sports jacket. Sewn beneath the magician were the initials *SWGM*.

Inside, Jamie aimed his stick at the cue ball and took his shot. All fifteen balls raced into holes, clearing the table. Jamie was the instant winner.

"All right, that was just dumb," said Darren. "You can't

cheat like that and get away with it."

"Cheat? Who cheated?"

"*You* did, cheater! You told the balls to go in the pockets, and they did!"

"How do you know?"

"Because I'm not an idiot, that's how I know!"

"Man, I can't pull *anything* over on you."

Darren sighed and shook his head as the doorbell rang.

"Who's that?" asked Jamie.

"How do I know? Why don't you answer it?"

Jamie gave a shrug and walked back out to the atrium, followed by Darren.

"Who is it?" Jamie shouted.

Outside the door, Wilson pressed a button on an intercom. His voice was broadcast over a speaker inside. "My name is Lance Wilson. I represent The Society of the World's Greatest Magicians."

Jamie looked at the speaker, then at Darren. "How did he do that?"

"He pushed a button, man. Let him in."

"Oh!" said Jamie, and he opened the door, revealing a tall, smiling, though kind of creepy-looking man. Darren thought his face had seen better days, like maybe when the guy was four. They all exchanged hellos.

"Sorry to bother you, gentlemen," said Wilson. "I know how busy you must be, but I've come with some very important and exciting news from our headquarters. May I come in?"

"Sure, sure," said Darren, motioning him in. "Uh, can we

get you something? We've got a housekeeper around somewhere who can, uh, conjure up anything you'd like. Heh, heh."

"Oh, a glass of water would be nice. Can we sit and talk?"

"How did you get that scar on your face?" blurted Jamie, much to Darren's dismay.

"Which one?" replied Wilson with a smirk.

Darren laughed and slapped Jamie hard on the arm. Jamie, realizing his rudeness, guffawed with gusto.

Darren called for Inga to bring them water and sodas. She replied from upstairs, "I am taking a brek! Go ged eet yourselfs!" Darren shook his head and went to retrieve the refreshments.

They brought Wilson into the huge, cavernous library. It was three levels high with polished mahogany shelves, complete with circular stairwells and stepladders.

"Beautiful library," said Wilson, his voice echoing, "but isn't it kind of empty?" Indeed, every shelf was bare.

"Oh, we just moved in," explained Jamie. "I forgot to bring my book."

"Ah," said Wilson, not sure if Jamie was joking. (He wasn't.) "Well, why don't I tell you why I've come?"

They sat on crisp, brown leather couches, and Wilson opened his case. He removed a few papers, followed by a golden statuette in the shape of a rabbit in a top hat. A gold plate on its base bore the inscription, *Jackson & Jenks, Members of SWGM.*

"Sweet!" said Jamie.

"On behalf of The Society of the World's Greatest Magicians, I want to congratulate you both. In the entire history of magic, there have been only fourteen performers admitted into this very exclusive and secret club. You gentlemen are now, as a team, the fifteenth candidates ever to be, uh, *considered* for this very important organization."

"Whoa!" Jamie exclaimed.

"Just fill out these forms with your address and phone numbers."

Jamie immediately scribbled the information, but Darren was skeptical. "Wait a minute," he said. "Why is this club so important?"

"Why?" replied Wilson. "Well, because, uh, you and the others represent the very best that magic has ever offered the world. And this is a way to make sure you have everything you need to keep your careers on track and running smoothly."

"Uh-huh, and who are the others?" Darren grilled further.

Wilson read a list from an index card. "Well, we're talking about Houdini, Kellar, Thurston, The Blackstones, Mark Wilson, David Copperfield, Doug Henning, The Amazing Ozlo—"

"Wow, Ozlo's in it!" exclaimed Jamie. "Do you think we'll get to meet him?"

"Well, he'd really like to meet *you*, so yes, that's entirely possible," smirked Wilson as he slipped Jamie's information into his case. "Word has it that he's a big fan of yours."

"Did you hear that, Darren? The Amazing Ozlo is a fan of ours!"

"Yeah, yeah, yeah," said Darren dismissively. "But now, Mr., uh, Wilson, you said we were only *candidates* for this club."

"Yes, so far that is the case."

"Well, what do we need to do to be in it?" asked Jamie.

"That is a very good question."

"Thanks!" exclaimed Jamie, enthralled by the compliment.

Wilson continued. "All the really great magicians keep secrets—at least a few particular tricks and illusions that they have never, and *will* never share with anyone outside the organization." Wilson pulled a large manila envelope from his case. "This envelope contains those very secrets. Many have tried to steal these irreplaceable documents over the years, but all have failed."

"And what does this have to do with us?" asked Darren.

"All the magicians in the society have first shown their willingness to participate by revealing a few of their favorite effects—particularly the ones that other magicians might not be familiar with."

"And so you want us to tell you how we do our tricks," continued Darren, smelling a rat.

"Only if you want to be in the organization. It's strictly up to you, of course. And in return, you will have the honor of being one of the few members of an elite organization that has stood the test of time. So . . . who would like to start?"

Darren had heard enough. "Well, I'm sorry, but I don't think—"

"We were at a thrift shop a few months ago when this guy walked up to me and—"

"Jamie, no! We're not telling him anything."

"Why not?" asked Jamie.

"Because we're just not. I don't think it's a very good idea."

"But we'll get to meet The Amazing Ozlo!"

Wilson was growing nervous, but kept his cool. "Look, why don't I step out of the room while you discuss this, and—"

"No, that's it, Mr. Wilson," concluded Darren. "We're not telling our secrets, so the organization will just have to do without us for now."

"I'm . . . very sorry to hear that," said Wilson. "The officers' panel will be shocked and upset. Magicians throughout the ages have *begged* us to get in. No one has ever turned down an outright *offer*."

"Well, looks like we're the first, then," said Darren. He stood, indicating the meeting was over. "Sorry. Thank you for your time."

"But, uh, well, wait a minute," said Wilson, breaking a sweat. "Did I tell you about the money?" He had no intention of going back to Ozlo without the boys' secrets.

"What money?" asked Jamie.

"Just for joining the organization, I'm hereby appointed to give you a check for four hundred thousand dollars. That's enough to build a whole new show for your next TV special."

"Wow, Darren!" said Jamie. "That's a lot of money!"

Darren was stunned by the sum, but he had a strong feeling that something was very wrong. "No, I still don't think so, but thanks anyway."

"Sheesh!" said Jamie. "Well, you'd be disappointed anyway, Mr. Wilson. We don't really know how we do the tricks." Jamie missed Darren's sharp glare aimed squarely in his direction. "I just say things like, 'Glass, serve me the last sip of soda,' and it just happens, like this . . ."

Jamie's glass levitated from the table and hovered near his face. He opened his mouth and the glass tipped toward it, feeding him its contents. Wilson observed the event with wide-eyed interest.

Darren tried to bring the impromptu performance to a swift conclusion. "Okay, well, that was one of our newest tricks that we'll be doing when—"

"Then I might say, 'Fly around, glass,'" interrupted Jamie, "and *look*. . . ."

Without a beat, the glass sailed skyward and zipped around the room. Wilson was astounded.

"Jamie!" said Darren. Seeing there was no stopping him, Darren tried to appease Wilson. "Careful now—don't want to ruin the, uh, magnets. Yeah, it's all done with magnets, see, hidden all around the room. Clever, huh? Bring 'er in now, pal."

"Okay," said Jamie. "But first, I might also say, 'Glass, fill the room with books!'"

"Jamie, no!" pleaded Darren.

But the glass, seeming to take on a life of its own, shot up to a third-level bookcase and turned toward the shelves. A shocking blue and white ray suddenly blazed from its mouth. It made an eerie high-pitched whistle while, slowly and clearly, books appeared on the shelves, beneath the ray's gleam.

Wilson was dumbstruck. Darren, though nervous, couldn't help but marvel at the spectacle himself. Jamie smiled, enjoying it all.

The glass glided along the upper deck of the library, and books of all shapes and sizes morphed into view wherever its blinding ray made contact. It gradually picked up speed, as if building confidence in its book-birthing abilities. By the time the glass reached the bottom floor of shelves, it was shooting along like a bottle rocket.

Twenty seconds later, the entire room overflowed with books. Mission accomplished, the glass flew back and came to a gentle rest on the coffee table, right in front of Wilson. Then, apparently not finished, the glass bolted upward and turned upside-down, hovering above the table. Wilson slowly reached out and ran his hand all around it. Suddenly, the ray shot out from its mouth, causing Wilson to jerk back with a yelp. The three shielded their eyes as two stacks of tabletop books appeared. The last was a picture book, *The Illustrated History of Drinking Glasses.* Mission accomplished, the glass came back to rest on the table.

Darren looked at Jamie. "Well, I see you've been practicing that one. It's, uh, really coming along, heh, heh. The kid's got talent, don't you think, Wilson?"

Wilson, observing the completely furnished library, appeared to be in shock. His eyes saw what happened, but his brain refused to believe it. "Thawas . . . Ih went . . . The thing jus . . . I saw, ih . . ." He stared at the boys, mouth agape, then suddenly bolted from the room.

"Mr. Wilson!" Jamie shouted. The two scurried after him.

"Hey, come back!" yelled Darren.

But Wilson wasn't about to return. He flung open the front doors and sprinted down the steps to his car. The boys watched from the door, surprised at how frightened this intimidating-looking man had become.

"Wilson, wait!" said Darren.

Wilson floored the gas pedal. The tires screeched and the car sped. The driveway gate crawled open, much too slowly for the panicked man. He barreled toward it, and *crash*—his bumper plowed into the wrought iron. The heavy car busted right through it, decimating the bars.

The boys winced as the car raced down the street and out of sight. They heard the final sound of squealing tires at the end of the block. Darren gave Jamie an angry, accusing look. Jamie returned a sheepish gaze.

"Do you think this means we're not in the club?"

Darren shook his head and sighed.

CHAPTER 11

Ozlo Awaits

OZLO was even more frustrated than the day before as he (for the thirty-eighth time) rewound and watched the finale of the boys' TV special. They stood in front of the Leaning Tower of Pisa in Italy and announced that they were going to make the building stand straight. Jamie gave the command, and, as advertised, the structure creaked, twisted, groaned, and raised itself to a perfect vertical position. The audience at the site applauded wildly.

"It's just not . . . possible!" Ozlo grumbled to himself. He had hardly slept the night before. His long straight hair was strung out like a wet mop, and fleshy bags drooped under his tired, bloodshot eyes.

A built-in speaker over the bedroom doorway emitted a soothing electronic female voice—"Lance Wilson is entering the compound."

"Wilson!" said Ozlo.

He ran to the balcony window and looked down to the huge, lushly landscaped courtyard entrance. A wide cobblestone driveway wrapped around an elaborate stone fountain. Streams of water showered from a larger-than-life sculpture of Ozlo himself, complete with flowing cape and magic wand. (A team of workers was carefully dismantling a sculpture of Nadine from the same fountain.)

Wilson's car came into view.

"Finally!" said Ozlo. He sat in a leopard-skin chair and turned on the TV news, preparing to pretend that any information about the boys was no longer a big deal.

A minute later, Wilson knocked and entered.

"Oh, hello, Wilson," said Ozlo in a calm, friendly voice. "How was the flight back? Did my crew treat you well?"

Wilson was still quite shaken by what he'd witnessed. "Uh . . . ih . . . uh . . ."

"Good, good," said Ozlo, oblivious to the man's odd state. He turned down the volume on the TV. "Well, I couldn't make out what you were saying either time we tried to speak. *Terrible* connection, those phones. Now, tell me—"

"The books were . . . *No* books, and it . . . They . . . The glass rose, and . . . Library empty . . . Ih . . . uh . . ."

"Uh-huh. Well, this is *still* a bad connection, and I'm standing right here. Are you okay, or did something—"

"The library was empty, I . . . I saw it. Yes. I did."

"You saw their library. Fine. So, uh, they're not big readers, huh? What else did you find out?"

Wilson looked at him and said plainly, "Nothing."

"Nothing?" asked Ozlo, his voice slightly louder. "How could you have found out nothing? Didn't the plan work? The magic society, the money?

"They . . . have spells of some kind. They're . . . freaks or, I don't know . . . witches."

"Witches."

"Yes."

Ozlo could no longer hide his exasperation. He stood up and yelled in the man's face. "There are no witches! There's only magicians who do magic tricks! Now, how did they do them? What did they tell you?"

"Freaks," was all Wilson replied, sounding a lot like the freshly insane Tad Le Vine. "Wizards."

"Wizards. I see," said Ozlo, nodding pensively. He then grabbed Wilson by his lapels. Normally, grabbing a man like Wilson would be a grave error, but Ozlo was desperate, and Wilson seemed to be in some sort of trance. "*They're not wizards or witches, Wilson! They're little snot-nosed kids, and they're doing these tricks somehow! Now, tell me right now what they—*" He stopped abruptly, seeing his own picture on the TV news next to a photo of the President of the United States. "Hey, look, it's me!"

He rushed to the remote and cranked the volume. An attractive black female news anchor said, "For the past eight years, The Amazing Ozlo has appeared at the White House, performing for all of the First Family's birthday celebrations.

Here he is last year with five-year-old Paulina."

A video showed a beaming Ozlo posing with the President's cute-as-a-button daughter. He held a top hat, out of which popped a rabbit. The child was amazed and delighted.

"You see that, Wilson?" said Ozlo proudly. "*Now* tell me who's the greatest magician in the—"

"But for *this* year's birthday," the anchor continued, "Paulina has personally requested the new, astounding magic team of Jackson and Jenks instead."

The screen filled with a clip from the boys' TV special. They again made the Leaning Tower of Pisa stand up straight.

"Step aside, Amazing Ozlo," the anchor joked. "This pair makes *Houdini* look like an amateur. No word yet on the incredible team's response to the request. But sources say their agent is negotiating a deal for the magical duo to—"

Smash! A heavy chair, hurled by an enraged Ozlo, busted through the center of the screen. Wires sparked and pieces flew.

"*Noooooooo! Noooooooo!*" bellowed Ozlo. "This will not stand! Do you hear me? *This will not stand!*" He emitted a primal roar and heaved a standing lamp at the screen.

Wilson looked on, slowly feeling renewed confidence. His next assignment from Ozlo was sure to be closer to his particular field of expertise: physical intimidation.

CHAPTER 12

Ozlo's Revenge

DARREN lugged a box of clothing toward the immense staircase in his new mansion. On his way past the kitchen, he peaked in and did a double take—a huge mess covered the expanse of granite countertops. The fridge had been raided, sandwiches prepared, drinks poured, desserts devoured, and nothing had been cleaned or put away. Darren groaned, thinking that this *Inga* was not particularly great at anything as far as he could tell.

His annoyance turned to curiosity as he heard sounds of yelling and splashing. Darren entered the kitchen, laid down the box, and peered out the back window. There, having a great time in the pool, were Jamie and Inga. Jamie threw her a beach ball, and she screamed and swam away from him. Jamie dove toward her and knocked it out of her hands. She squealed with delight.

"You cannod haff de bowl!" she shouted, racing back over to it.

Darren stormed over to the back door and strode out to the pool. "What are you guys doing?" he said snarkily.

"We're playing water polo!" replied Jamie. "Come on in, Darren! We'll have a tag-team match!"

"I'm not comin' anywhere. There's a big mess in the kitchen."

"I vill clin it op if he vins zee bettle."

"Zee bettle?" said Darren.

"Yas, he mossed get de bowl again, ah, seffen more times. Yoo-hoo, megic boy! Eet looks lige I'fe got zee bowl!"

Jamie heaved a monstrous growl, and she screamed and splashed away. She grabbed the side of the pool, near Darren.

"Deed you know dat he vas real megic?" Inga asked Darren.

"Uh . . . What do you mean exactly," said a worried Darren.

"He med me float erount here lige eh beeg fet balloon!"

"*You told her?*" Darren barked at Jamie. "And you made her *float?*"

"We were just having some fun," said Jamie.

"Man, you can't do that!"

"Oh, don't worry. She won't tell anyone, will you, Inga?"

"I don't dell nothink to no one. Besites, he said he vould durn me into ah beeg green monster if I deed."

"See?" said Jamie. "Oh, uh . . . stuff in the kitchen, clean yourself up!" Through the kitchen window, Darren witnessed the raucous clatter of self-cleaning and straightening. Inga laughed and clapped while Darren shook his head.

Jamie's cell phone rang, and he hopped out of the pool and answered it. "Hello? . . . Yes. . . . Yes. . . . Okay, what's the address? . . . Five Hundred West Thirty-second Street. . . . Okay, I'll be there as soon as I can." He hung up.

"What was that all about?" asked Darren.

"Oh, it was the dry cleaners. They said I had to come pick up our stuff before the end of the day. They're closing down for remodeling."

"I thought Ainsley was picking up the dry cleaning."

"Well, maybe he forgot. Too busy booking us gigs. I'll just go get it. Hey, I can zap myself over there!"

"Yeah, sure, whatever," said Darren, feeling jealous. Not only could Jamie do real magic, but Inga obviously liked him. She was very pretty, Darren thought—though, if possible, a dimmer bulb than Jamie.

"Eef you go, den I am ze wiener!" announced Inga. "I'm ze wiener! I'm ze wiener!"

Jamie laughed. "Yep, you're ze wiener, Inga! I'll be back soon." He walked into the house.

Inga rested her arms poolside. "He's real megic," she stated again. Darren just sighed.

Jamie threw on some clothes in his room, then repeated the dry cleaner's address and ordered himself to go there. Instantly, he vanished.

A minute later, Ainsley showed up at the door with an armful of garments in plastic bags.

"Hi, there!" he said excitedly. "Have you guys been watching the news?"

"No," said Darren. "What happened?"

"*You're* what happened! President Brady wants you and Jamie to perform at his daughter's birthday party next month. He requested you personally!"

"No! For real? I mean for *real*, for real?"

"For real! You're going to the White House!"

"Wow!" yelled Darren. "The White House! Jamie's gonna freak!"

"Where is he?"

"The dry cleaners. They called his cell phone a little while ago." Then, thinking quickly: "He just, uh, took a taxi there."

Ainsley was confused. "But that's impossible."

"Why?"

"Because these are all your clothes right here."

"Oh. Did you just get them?"

"No, I picked them up this morning. Why would they tell him to come get clothes that weren't there anymore?"

"I don't know."

Ainsley thought for a moment. "What dry cleaner did he go to?"

Darren scrunched his brow, racking his brain to recall what Jamie had said. "Umm . . . I don't remember. I . . . Darn, I have no idea."

"Five Hundred West Thirty-second Street," chimed Inga, sashaying in from the kitchen with an ice-cream cone and a beach towel. She exited to the pool, leaving behind a mocking "Ha!"

"Uh, yeah, that was it," said Darren.

"Thirty-second . . . I think there's just a bunch of old buildings there."

The two looked at each other, puzzled. Slowly, a look of realization came over them—Jamie might be in some sort of trouble.

"Let's go!" said Darren.

The two ran outside, jumped into Ainsley's new gold convertible sports car, and took off. There was no waiting for the gate to open—there was still a gaping hole where Wilson's car had busted through it.

"What happened to the gate?" asked Ainsley, zooming down the street.

"Oh, there was a guy here from a magic club, and Jamie scared him so bad, he bolted."

"How did he scare him?"

"He did some magic and the dude just freaked."

Ainsley smiled. "I'm not surprised. What magic club do you belong to?"

"We don't. He wanted to sign us up for one."

"Really?"

"Yeah. But first, he wanted us to tell him our secrets. I said no way."

"Huh," said Ainsley, pensively.

"What?"

"I'm not sure, but I have a feeling that the real trick may be on us."

Darren looked at Ainsley, realizing he was probably right.

"Let's get our butts over there," he said.

Ainsley sped up.

AT THE SAME MOMENT, a swirl of wind kicked up in back of an abandoned theater, and Jamie magically appeared in its center. "Whew!" he said. He had been unable to see or hear anything in the few minutes it took him to travel through space. It was actually pretty scary, he thought. He made a mental note to never do it again.

He looked at the building—wooden boards, sloppily hammered across the doors and windows, were suffering from dry rot and fatigue. Jamie rechecked the address. Funny place for a dry cleaning joint, he thought. No wonder they were closing to remodel.

He walked up to the backstage door. A white cardboard sign with *Bing's Laundry,* scrawled in red magic marker, was taped to it, along with an arrow pointing to the doorknob. Jamie shrugged and entered.

He walked down a dark, dirty, smelly, cobweb-filled corridor. Faded, dog-eared posters of bands and shows clung to the walls. Every few yards, another bright red arrow pointed the way, though the appearance of a dry cleaning facility seemed an increasingly unlikely possibility.

"Man, this cleaners needs a cleaner," Jamie muttered to himself. He finally spied an open door with a light shining inside. "Hello? Bing's Laundry?"

"Yes, in here," said a voice.

"I just gotta say," said Jamie, turning into the room, "you guys win the prize for creepiest dry cleaning . . ." He stopped short, noticing a few odd things at once. The first was a tall, fat Asian man in a black jacket and dark shades standing before him, arms folded. "Oh, hey," said Jamie, "you go here, too? That outfit looks very nicely pressed." Second, he noticed that he was in a dusty dressing room with nothing to suggest that it was, or had ever been, a dry cleaning shop. "Where's all the clothes?" he wondered aloud. "Oh, man, I got here too late! We've got to wait until the whole place is finished!"

Then the door closed.

Sitting in a decaying brown leather chair was The Amazing Ozlo. Wilson stood firmly behind him.

"The Amazing Ozlo! And Mr. Wilson!" said Jamie. "Hey, hey! You're the last people I ever expected to find here. It must be, like, a *private* cleaners for rich and famous people, huh? This is great—I've always wanted to meet you, Ozlo!"

"And I've been wanting to meet you, my friend," said Ozlo sincerely. "You and your partner are really very great magicians."

A realization hit Jamie. "Aaaaah, now I get it. This is the initiation into the club!" He laughed loudly. "For a second there, I thought this was actually some sort of dry cleaning joint!"

Ozlo looked at Wilson, not quite believing that someone as talented as Jamie was also just as stupid as Wilson had suggested.

"Yes, that's it," said Ozlo, playing along. "Welcome to the initiation."

"I'm sorry Darren's missing this," said Jamie, "but actually, I don't think he was too thrilled by the whole idea. He can go a bit heavy on the, you know, lame-itude sometimes. We'll just keep that to ourselves, though, huh?"

"Ah, then you're the one we want," said Ozlo, smiling. "So . . . I loved the special."

"Thanks!" said Jamie.

"I was especially impressed by the opening, with the legs jumping out of the box and dancing. Very nicely done."

"Yeah, I thought that one up. Pretty good stuff, huh?"

"Yes, yes. So . . . how did you do it?"

"How did I do . . ."

"The illusion. How did you do it?"

"Well, to tell you the truth, Ozlo, I don't really know. In fact, we usually just make them all up right on the spot."

The smile slowly left Ozlo's face, and the large Asian man stepped closer to Jamie.

"Hi, there," said Jamie. "I don't think we've met."

"That's Pauly," Ozlo interceded. "He's always around to make sure that I get . . . exactly what I want."

"*Very* cool. Well, hey, any friend of Ozlo's is a friend of mine," said Jamie. He extended his hand for a shake, but Pauly didn't budge.

"He's a man of few words," explained Ozlo. "Have a seat." He motioned to Pauly, who moved a chair over to Jamie.

"Oh, thanks," said Jamie, sitting. He then wondered why Pauly planted himself up against the chair—until it dawned on him. "Oh!" He whipped out his wallet, fished for a dollar, and held it out. "Sorry, I'm really new to tipping everybody. Is that, like, enough?"

"He doesn't want your money," said Ozlo. "He wants you to tell me how you do your tricks."

"Ah. Well, it's sort of, uh . . . It's kinda hard to say."

"Well, perhaps you should give it a try. Just say whatever comes to mind and we'll sort it all out afterwards."

"Oh. . . . Oh, waaaaaaait a minute, I get it," said Jamie, actually getting it. "You want me to tell you so that you can do the tricks yourself!"

"Not really, but why shouldn't I, if that's what I want to do?" snipped Ozlo. "You can just make some more up on the spot, can't you?"

Wilson moved to the other side of Jamie's chair. Jamie, feeling very uncomfortable, started to get up.

"Well, hey, I've really enjoyed meeting you and your friends, Ozlo, but . . ." Pauly shoved him back down. "What?" screeched Jamie. "What the . . ."

Ozlo turned deadly serious. "Okay, listen, punk, and listen good. I'm tired of you two stealing my spotlight and taking my jobs. Now, either you tell me how you do those tricks or I'll see to it that you never perform again—for anyone!"

Jamie couldn't believe his ears. The Amazing Ozlo himself was sitting right in front of him, threatening him with . . . something that didn't sound particularly nice.

"All right, that's it!" announced Jamie. "I am not joining any club! You can just forget it! If this is the kind of initiation we're expected to put up with, you can just pack up and go home!"

Ozlo and Wilson exchanged an incredulous look. Ozlo decided to switch tactics.

"I see," he said. "I apologize for my rudeness. You want me to reveal some of *my* tricks first. Okay, then, fair enough." Ozlo reached into his pocket and pulled out a large shiny coin attached to a string. "Keep your eye on this coin," he said, letting it dangle. "It's got very magical properties." Unseen by Jamie, Wilson pulled out an electronic syringe.

"Oh, you're going to try to hypnotize me, huh?" said Jamie. "Well, you can just forget that, too. I can't believe you'd think I'd be stupid enough to—" Wilson pressed the syringe against Jamie's arm, pressed a button, and *pop*—Jamie was injected. He instantly fell limp, his head dropping backward. "—vawl ver an old one like dsadsth," he sputtered.

"Sit him up," ordered Ozlo. The men tried to comply, but Jamie's lithe, rubbery body managed to slither from their hands.

"Ayyy, you are good," said Jamie, experiencing his sudden jelly-like state. "You'll have to teash me how to hippo-tize like thad." His head clunked on the metal seat, his body splayed out in front of him. "Ceilings, ooh, ooh, ooh," he sang. "Nothing more than ceilings." The men finally succeeded in sitting him up.

"Okay, then. Jamie. Jamie, it's Ozlo."

"Ossssloooo. So good to meed yooooz. Youze are the zecond greatest magician in the whole worldzzzzzzz. No, waits—the third. Darren made milk shoot out of a tube."

Ozlo's nostrils flared. "Listen to me, Jamie. You feel yourself wanting to tell the truth now, don't you?"

"The troooonts."

"Yes, the truth, that's it. I'm going to ask you some questions and you are going to tell me the answers—the *complete* answers. Do you understand?"

"Thez anzerzzz, yezz. Completely thee anzerzzz."

"Excellent. Here we go. How did you do the first illusion in your TV special?"

Ozlo leaned forward, anxious to learn the secrets at last.

AINSLEY TURNED onto Thirty-second Street and looked for the address. Seeing that the neighborhood was run-down with many boarded-up, graffiti-covered buildings, he grew increasingly nervous.

"And then this Wilson guy said something about Ozlo wanting to meet us," said Darren, trying to come up with any helpful clues.

"Ozlo, of course! Why didn't I think of that before?"

"What *about* Ozlo?"

"He *must* be behind this."

"Why would you think that?"

"Well . . . all I'll say is that I know him. Or rather, I *knew* him. I . . . I tried to sign him to the agency once."

"You did? When?"

"Many years ago. I told him he might be as great and famous a magician as Harry Houdini one day."

"Yeah, and what did he say?" asked Darren.

"He threw me against a wall. He shook his fist in my face and said, 'Houdini was nothing compared to me! I'm already better than that two-bit piece of garbage!'"

"Oh, my God! What did you do?"

"Nothing. I was shocked. I just let him storm away."

"Now *that* is bizarre. But why would he go after Jamie?"

"Ozlo is a violent ego-maniac, always having to be thought of as the best, even if it means roughing someone up. Can you imagine what he thinks of you two? And you just took over his White House gig—I can't imagine he's too thrilled about that. I'm willing to bet that he'd try to force Jamie to give away your secrets, at the very least!"

"I can't believe that! *Ozlo?*"

"Believe it."

"Step on it, man. If he finds out the truth, we're through."

"The truth?"

"Uh, I mean the secrets. If he finds out the secrets."

JAMIE continued muttering incoherently as the serum took further effect. "And then the man who's in the thriff sorz, and he says I am a meanie. I gives you threez minishas."

"Speak clearer," ordered Ozlo. "I can't understand a word you're saying!"

"I'm hymmonized, I'm do anybing you dzay. Your fish is my con man."

"You idiot!" Ozlo barked at Wilson. "You gave him too much serum!"

"Give it a few minutes," Wilson replied. "It'll wear off a bit."

"I don't have a few minutes!" He knelt in front of Jamie. "Jamie, now listen to me. Start again and speak slowly and clearly. How did you do the first trick?"

"Oh, very well, thang you. It was quide a goob trig, huh-ya?"

Ozlo let out a frustrated groan and wiped the sweat from his brow. He waited a few minutes and questioned him again. This time, Jamie spoke more clearly.

"We were . . . in a thrift shop," he began.

AINSLEY drove up and parked behind the theater. The two saw the sign next to the door.

"A dry cleaners, huh?" said Ainsley. "Only a complete bonehead would mistake this dump for a dry cleaners."

"Yep, and I know just the bonehead. We have to go in there and save him."

"Oh, now-now-now wait a minute," stuttered Ainsley. "I, I didn't say anything about going in there. Let's call the police."

"There's no time! Besides, it's just Ozlo. What could he possibly do to us?"

Ainsley just looked at him sheepishly.

"Fine!" said Darren. "I'll go in there myself. Just keep the car running."

Darren got out and entered the building.

JAMIE spilled the entire story, piece by piece. "And then . . . when I said for my dog to disappear . . . it really did. And then it came back when I said for it to . . . reappear."

"Because of this, this *genie?*" said Ozlo, trying to make sense of it all.

"Yes. The genie. From another galaxy . . . somewhere. It left me with the power to do anything I want to do."

"Really? Anything? Make me disappear."

Wilson, who figured by now that Jamie could do it, reacted strongly. "Uh, Ozlo, I really think you should have him hold off on that."

"Oh, you think it's possible, huh? Okay, kid, make *Wilson* disappear."

Ozlo laughed as Wilson stammered nervously. "Uh, ih, ahhh—"

The door burst open, startling the men. Darren strode in, ready for action. "Ozlo, it *is* you!" he said. "Okay, give him up. He's got no business here."

"Well, well, well, if it isn't the super-power-free half of the team," said Ozlo smugly. "I was hoping I'd get to meet you. Someone's got to fill me in on the details of this cool genie bottle story."

"Forget it. Let's go, Jamie. We're getting out of here."

"Yeah, you wish!" said Ozlo. "He'll be staying with me for a while."

"Yes, go," replied Jamie, catching a second wind of his serum-driven stupor. "Less all go nowz."

"You *drugged* him?"

"It's just a little truth serum," said Ozlo. "And what's that they say?—The truth shall set you free."

Ozlo motioned to his men and they grabbed Darren. As he struggled to escape, he finally noticed Wilson.

"*You?*"

"Last I checked," sneered Wilson, grasping Darren's arm and shoulder. "You should have taken the money, kid."

Darren realized Ainsley was right about Ozlo. He was as much a cheap thug as he was a magician. He and his men scared Darren, but he knew he had no choice—he had to act tough and escape with Jamie.

"Let me go!" he demanded.

"They'll release both of you just as soon as I know what I want to know," said Ozlo matter-of-factly. "I went through all this trouble, after all. You can't expect me to fly all the way back home with nothing up my sleeve."

"I'm not telling you anything, Ozlo!" said Darren. "You might as well give up and let us out of here!"

"Yeah, you wish!"

"You seem to like saying that," mocked Darren.

"I think you'll tell us everything," continued Ozlo. "Wilson, you got any more of that serum?"

"Yes," he replied, removing the syringe from his pocket.

"Jamie," said Darren, "now wouldn't be a bad time for a little you-know-what."

"Wha, like some dessert?" asked Jamie, unable to make much sense. "Sorry, there's no more Jell-O."

Wilson removed the syringe and pressed a button to reset it.

"Yeah, Jell-O, Jell-O," said Darren, thinking fast. "Their arms are like Jell-O."

Jamie was confused. "Whose arms are like—"

"Wilson and this guy. Say that their arms are like Jell-O."

"Wilson and Pauly's arms are like Jell-O?"

"Don't ask it—say it!" demanded Darren. Wilson aimed the syringe at Darren's arm.

"Wilson and Pauly's arms are like Jell-O!" said Jamie.

And it was so. The henchmen's arms went completely limp. The syringe plunked to the floor as their hands fell helplessly to their sides, freeing Darren.

"I . . . I can't move my arms!" yelled a panicked Pauly.

"Me, neither!" said Wilson. "They're, they're like rubber! *Now* do you believe me?" he squawked to Ozlo.

"I see it, but I don't believe it," replied Ozlo, completely mesmerized. The harder the men tried moving their arms, the more rubbery they became.

"Looks like our work here is done," said Darren, helping Jamie up and pulling an arm around his shoulder.

Ozlo started toward them. "Wait just a minute!"

"I wouldn't move another inch, Ozlo," threatened Darren. "He's got magic powers and he's not afraid to use them. And if you tell anyone about the genie . . . Well, just don't say anything and you won't have to find out. Come on, Jamie!"

They bolted from the room and headed down the hallway. Ozlo appeared behind them in the doorway.

"Oh, boys," he said calmly. The two turned back to Ozlo. "You may have my men hypnotized or something, but you'll never stop *me*." He called to his bodyguards, "Block their path! I'll do the rest!"

Wilson and Pauly sprinted into the hallway, their arms flapping about like fish on a hook. They rushed toward the boys as Ozlo refilled the syringe.

Darren tried moving Jamie faster, but, still drugged, he could only stumble along.

"Quick, Jamie—think of something to stop them with."

"Like what?"

"Anything!"

"Chicken fajitas, block their path!" yelled Jamie.

From out of nowhere, a truckload of fajita ingredients flew at the men. Onions, peppers, taco shells, guacamole, rice, chicken, and sour cream pelted their bodies and blocked their sight. With no arm power, they were defenseless against the onslaught. They continually tripped and struggled to stand back up. Soon, however, the action abated, and the men, covered with fajita messes, continued after them. They stumbled over the food, but regained their footing.

"We need something else!" said Darren. "Something bigger!"

"Cave Squirrels, help us!" yelled Jamie, adding, "Very *big* Cave Squirrels!"

Two gigantic male and female cartoon squirrels suddenly loomed in front of the men, who skidded to a stop, their eyeballs bulging. As on TV, the animals wore bright caveman clothes and wielded large wooden clubs. They spanned the width of the hallway, their heads almost to the ceiling.

"Get 'em, Sparky!" squeaked the female squirrel, and they jumped at the men, who retreated in terror, arms flailing.

The men sprinted past Ozlo, who, fiddling with the syringe, looked up just in time to see a cartoon club flying at his face. *Smack*—it whacked him hard, making him spin around like the squirrels' TV victims.

The female squirrel wound up her batting arm, and *bam*— she smacked Ozlo in the legs. Ozlo spun around in the air, his body a comical blur. He landed with a *thud* against the wall, completely dazed. Cartoon stars and birdies appeared, circling his head with *tweet-tweets* and *cuckoos*.

"Let's go eat acorns!" said the male squirrel.

"Yeah. *Big* acorns! Hee, hee!"

"Cave Squirrels, disappear!" said Jamie who, along with Darren, had stopped to marvel at the bizarre battle.

The squirrels vanished, leaving Ozlo splayed out on the floor, his eyes swimming upward. Darren and Jamie hurried out of the building.

"TELL ME WHAT HAPPENED!" yelled a delighted Ainsley as he pulled out of the parking lot with the boys in the back seat. "How did you get him out of there?"

"Oh, it was nothing," said Darren. "Sometimes you've just got to show 'em who's boss. I don't think they'll be bothering us again."

"I've got to hand it to you, Darren," said Ainsley. "You never cease to amaze me."

"Well, the main thing is, we got *this* guy back. Oh, hey, Jamie, guess what?"

"What?" Jamie eked out while grasping his stomach. The

serum had made him nauseous.

"We've got a show to do—for the President's daughter! We're going to the White House, buddy!"

"What do you think of that, Jamie?" asked Ainsley.

A sickly look came over Jamie's face. He leaned out the window and threw up with a grotesque "Auugocheeeyeeee- www!"

Darren and Ainsley grimaced as the car turned a corner and sped away.

THE NEXT DAY, in spite of everything, Jamie couldn't help feeling sorry for Ozlo. After all, Jamie thought, Ozlo had worked hard to achieve his fame, while Jamie's success came by way of a genie from outer space. He gave a magical order for the two bodyguards' floppy arms to return to normal, hoping that would ease Ozlo's mind. He decided not tell Darren. "He'd hit the ceiling if he knew I did that," he muttered to himself. He then chuckled, remembering when Darren's head actually *did* hit the ceiling.

CHAPTER 13

The Wind and
the White House

TWO WEEKS LATER, a gleaming, golden stretch limousine arrived at the boys' mansion to escort them to the White House. Their mothers took pictures and shared in the excitement.

Inga jumped up and down as the boys climbed into the limo. "Bye! Haff fun!" she yelled. "Jemmie can do anythink, you know," she blabbed to the ladies. "He's *real* megic!" The mothers smiled politely at the seemingly ignorant, childish housekeeper.

The whole world agreed that the boys were fantastic. Their TV special and White House appearance cemented their position as the greatest magicians in the world—perhaps the greatest ever. Jamie's old boss, Mike, and even Calvert from Jimmy Giraffe's, had watched in awe as their former charges made history. Mike had a photo of Jamie from *Time Magazine* framed on the wall in the convenience store, with *My Favorite Employee* written beneath it. "Did you see Jamie on TV last

143

night?" he'd ask everyone. The customers loved discussing the magicians' latest feats.

When the limo pulled up to the gate at 1600 Pennsylvania Avenue, to the estate the President and the First Family called home, the boys tried to appear calm. They'd passed the White House countless times, but now they were invited guests. Their whispered "Wow's!" and "Cool's!" revealed their sheer excitement.

Once inside the large, regal Entrance Hall, they looked about in awe. A hustle and bustle of energy filled the expanse, and they could almost feel the building's vast history breathing within its very walls.

A White House tour group, with about twenty visitors, was passing through. "Oh, here's a special surprise, ladies and gentlemen," said the gaunt, graying tour guide, pointing. "It's Vice President Howell on his way to the West Wing."

Just as they turned, a teenage girl spotted the boys behind her. "Look! It's Jackson and Jenks!" she squealed.

Every head in the group swung around, and a swell of shouting echoed throughout the room. "It's them!" they yelled, racing toward the duo. "It's Jackson and Jenks!"

The eager throng rushed at the boys, thrusting pads, pencils, and cameras in their faces. The two were overwhelmed as the crowd, one row shoved by the other, backed them up against a wall. A trio of security guards ran to the rescue.

"Move back, everyone!" they commanded. "Let the gentlemen through! Move back, please!"

"Come this way, ladies and gentlemen!" pleaded the tour guide, craning his neck to catch a glimpse of the magicians. "We have lots more to see. Please!" Darren and Jamie signed a final autograph as the crowd was led away.

"Sheesh!" said Jamie, straightening his handsome black sport jacket and slick lavender T-shirt. "You'd think we stood out or something!"

"Could just be my natural beauty," joked Darren.

They were greeted by an attractive Latino White House representative whose nametag read *Gloria*.

"I'm sorry about the mob," she said amiably. "Are you both okay?"

"Oh, sure," replied Darren. "Jamie and the President and I always have this problem."

She laughed, then led them up an elevator and down seven hallways to a small, intimate theater. Four male White House assistants lugged in the boys' trunks and boxes, which they brought along to make it appear as if they used normal props.

When Gloria left, Jamie uttered a command and their real equipment appeared, all in place and ready to go. Included was a colorful Chinese cabinet for the show's finale. They planned to have the President's daughter step inside of it, to be turned, momentarily, into a guinea pig. Jamie loved guinea pigs—he'd had one as a kid. "His name was Willard," he'd said when the boys were planning the show the week before. "He looked like a huge rat with no tail." Their only concern: The

First Daughter, Paulina, would really be a guinea pig for a few minutes. Wouldn't she tell everyone about the transformation? They finally decided that if she tried to explain, everyone would just laugh and remark about her vivid imagination.

Gloria poked her head into the room less than a minute after she had left. "Excuse me, but how long will it take you to . . ." She saw the stage filled with tricks, all set up. "How did you get ready so quick?" she exclaimed.

Darren thought fast. "Oh, if you think *that* was snappy, wait'll you see our quick getaway after you actually *see* the show," he quipped, chuckling. He nudged Jamie to chuckle as well.

"Oh. Ha!" offered Jamie.

"Anyway, we're ready whenever."

"Okay. I'll bring them in now," she said, smiling. "I'm already amazed!" She left to fetch the partiers.

"Hey, how about we give 'em a show they'll never forget?" said Darren.

"Works for me, Dr. D!"

"For Mosi?"

"For Mosi!"

They gave each other an energetic hand slap, shouting "Deal!"

Gloria, along with a White House photographer, escorted First Daughter Paulina and seventeen other children into the theater. Their behavior was the exact opposite of the Jimmy Giraffe crowd. The mood was almost somber as they shuffled in and silently took their seats. The young guests had all been instructed by their parents to be on their best quiet behavior, as it was a great and serious honor to be invited to this particular birthday party.

"Did somebody croak?" Darren whispered to Jamie.

"I'll handle this," said Jamie. He turned to the kids.

"Hi, you guys," he said loudly. "Why are you so quiet? Where do you think you are—the White House?" The kids chuckled. He marched about stiffly and spoke in a robotic voice. "Hello there, I'm in the White House, so I've got to be a robot! I am a White House robot! I am a White House robot! I am a White Hou-Hou-Hou-Hou-Hou . . ." He spun around, pretending to break down as the kids laughed hard, and the ice was broken.

Darren chuckled as well. *That was actually kind of . . . smart,* he thought. He gave Jamie a friendly slap on the back.

And then on with the show: birds materialized, changed colors, and disappeared; Maxwell appeared and transformed into a bowl of fish, which vanished in a puff of smoke; Maxwell reappeared, leaping from a clear bucket. The kids, especially the curly blond-haired Paulina, loved every minute and offered nonstop laughter and applause.

As Darren introduced the next effect, the back doors opened and three Secret Service men entered. Gloria, who was enjoying the show, conferred with them, then turned and said, "Excuse me, Jackson and Jenks, but another fan of yours would like to come watch." With that, President Brady himself strode into the room. A few members of his Cabinet followed and sat in back while the Secret Service men stood off to the side. Jamie and Darren were awestruck.

"Daddy!" Paulina yelled, running to him. He laughed and swept her up in his arms. The skirt of her yellow polka dotted dress swayed behind her.

"Happy Birthday, Sweet Pea! Are you enjoying the magicians?"

"Yes!" she shouted, hugging him hard. "They're the greatest!"

"Okay, let's sit and watch. Sorry to interrupt," he said to the boys. "I'm a big fan. Please go on with the show."

At first, however, the two magicians could barely speak in the presence of the President.

"Uh . . . no problem," said Darren. "Okay, uh . . . like I was, uh, saying, we are going to, uh . . . to . . . What *was* I saying, Jamie?"

Everyone laughed, and the show continued, with the two producing multitudes of items from underneath a cloth—flowers, lamps, chandeliers, and finally, a large quacking duck. The crowd screamed and clapped.

Finally, it was time for the finale. "And now, Jamie and I will attempt an amazing experiment. But because we've never done this before, we need someone to act as a guinea pig for us because we want to turn them into . . . a real guinea pig!"

Everyone gasped, and the kids' hands shot up, except for Paulina's.

"Hmm, who would like to assist us with this?" said Darren. "How about our beautiful birthday girl?"

The kids cheered and shouted, "Go, Paulina!" and "They want *you!*"

But although the pretty, petite Paulina was the President's daughter, she was very shy. She always preferred to stay home and read rather than to go out with eight Secret Service men in tow. She also disliked having her picture taken as *herself,* much less in the apparent form of a guinea pig.

"No, Paulina?" asked Darren.

"Go, honey. It'll be fun," said the President, but Paulina wouldn't budge from his lap.

"That's okay, Paulina," assured Jamie. "So, who wants to help us?"

The children's hands shot up again as they begged to be chosen.

"How about you, Mr. President?" suggested a Cabinet member. The other officials chuckled at the idea.

"No, I don't think so," said the President. "If these boys are against my tax plan, they might not change me back." More chuckling.

"Oh, don't worry about us, Mr. President," said Darren, and he waved a magic wand. "We can just change the tax plan."

The adults broke out laughing, none harder than the President.

"Would you mind assisting us?" continued Darren carefully.

"Who wants the President to come up and help?" shouted Jamie. The kids yelled and applauded their approval.

The President threw up his hands. "Well, why not?" he said, resting his daughter in a chair and rising. "I'd rather be a healthy guinea pig than a lame duck." The Cabinet men guffawed as the President strode to the front of the room.

"But Darren," whispered Jamie, "won't *he* tell everyone that he was actually turned into a guinea pig?"

"Not if he wants to finish out his term."

"Oh. Yeah. Okay."

The President, who stood a towering six-feet three-inches tall, shook the boys' hands and asked how he could be of assistance. Jamie wheeled the colorful cabinet to the front while Darren explained the effect. The President would step inside, and *presto-chango,* he would appear to be a guinea pig. They'd then close the door, say the magic word, and he would be the President once again.

"Sounds fine to me," said the President amiably. "What do I do?"

Everyone, including the Secret Service men, smiled with anticipation as President Brady stepped into the cabinet. He had to kneel down and wriggle his body to fit inside.

"I think this thing was *made* for a guinea pig," he joked, causing more laughter.

"See you soon, Mr. President!" said Darren. They shut the cabinet door, and Darren latched it with a metal spike.

"Turn into a guinea pig!" commanded Jamie as the two

wheeled the cabinet once around. Darren knocked on the door.

"Mr. President?" No response. Darren gave a comical shrug and knocked again. "Are you in there, Mr. President?" Again, nothing. "Hmm, maybe we should check and see what happened, huh, kids?"

"Yes!" they shouted.

Jamie unlatched the door and swung it open. The President was indeed gone, and in his place was a plump tan and white guinea pig. It looked about, its nose in a constant twitch. Its movements were quick and jerky, and it had a face like a beaver, with a prominent pair of buckteeth.

"Ladies and gentlemen, I give you President Brady, the guinea pig!" crowed Darren, and the room broke out in laughter and applause.

Kids and adults alike leaned forward to get a good look at the animal. The Secret Service and the Cabinet members conferred among themselves, trying to guess where the President had actually gone. There had to be a trap door, they figured, or maybe he was behind the box. They were all thrilled to participate in a moment of fun during their normal hectic workday.

Darren, meanwhile, was very worried when Jamie scooped up the guinea pig in his hands. It was one thing to turn the most powerful man in the free world into a three-and-a-half pound rodent, but toying with him and risking injury was too much for him to stomach.

"Uh, careful with that, Amazing Jamie," said Darren, forcing a chuckle. "Wouldn't want to hurt the *President of the United States* now, would we?"

"I *am* being careful," said Jamie, "but look how cute he is! Isn't he cute, kids?" The children voiced their agreement. Paulina, delighted, pressed her hands against her giggling mouth.

"Well, it's time to turn the cute little pipsqueak back into the President," said Darren, anxious to bring the trick to a speedy conclusion.

"Yay!" the kids yelled, but Jamie held the animal up to his face.

"Oh, yes you *are* a cute guinea pig," he said childishly. "You are the cutest little thing I've ever seen, yes you are!" He gave the guinea pig a loud kiss on the head, and the kids shrieked with laughter.

Darren quickly and carefully lifted the rodent from Jamie's hands. "Jamie, could you at least *pretend* to be a normal person?" he said as he placed the animal back into the cabinet, shut the door, and secured the latch.

"Hey, I wish I *was* a normal person," replied Jamie. "Then I'd—"

He wasn't able to finish his sentence.

A sudden gust of wind blasted the back doors wide open with a startling *bang*.

"*Nooooooooooooooo!*" cried Darren, but the sweeping, wailing gale force drowned out his voice.

The children screamed with fright while the Secret Service men bolted from their seats.

"Everbody down!" shouted one.

Panicked, all hit the deck as the men drew guns and ducked behind chairs, struggling to assess the situation. One man tried running to the doors, but the vicious wind held him firmly back. Another dashed toward the Chinese cabinet, and the wind blew him down like he was made of feathers.

Darren, flattened against a wall, knew full well what this meant, but hoped against hope that he was wrong. Jamie hugged a beam for balance.

The wind then halted. All was silent.

"Stay down! Nobody move!" barked the head Secret Service man. He sent quick hand signals to the other two—one ran out the doors, gun drawn, looking for anyone or anything suspicious. The fallen man leaped up and ran to the cabinet, shoving Darren out of his way. He tried opening the door, but couldn't get the latch to budge. Darren said, "Wait," and properly unhooked it. All eyes faced front.

A feeling of dread came over Jamie. He closed his eyes and quickly muttered, "The President is back to his original form."

Everyone sat up, anticipating the return of their leader. Darren opened the door.

There was only the guinea pig.

CHAPTER 14

Special Agent Stonewell

JAMIE AND DARREN sat alone in a small dining room a floor above the theater. Jamie just stared into space. Darren was bent forward, his head adrift in his hands. He heaved a sigh and looked up at a clock on the wall. It had been a little over two hours since the unthinkable had occurred.

The unthinkable: Jamie accidentally used his final wish, and it was to turn himself back into an ordinary person, with no magical powers to speak of. The President of the United States was now a small furry creature, and all the "Abracadabras" in the world would not change him back.

The immediate aftermath of the show had been a nightmare. The alarmed children were quickly ushered from the room while the Secret Service tore the Chinese cabinet apart. Their panic peaked when they found no sign of the President. The boys were taken upstairs and grilled for information. They spilled everything they knew about the genie. They explained to the Secret Service, White House Security, the FBI, the CIA, and the Vice President that they, quite frankly, could not perform a single magic trick that required any actual talent. Jamie was given supernatural powers and now they were gone, most likely for good. The panel was skeptical of their fantastic story, but with no other explanations to consider, they left to plan their next move.

The animal itself was being held in a secret room under the strictest supervision. No one but the boys believed the little critter was President Brady, but no one completely rejected the idea, either. Until the President turned up, no stone would be left unturned; no idea ruled out.

Ten minutes after the incident, the Vice President was secretly sworn in as Interim President, taking over for the time being, but only a few were briefed about the crisis. It had been quickly decided that only the highest ranking government officials, a few trusted aides, and the FBI and CIA would be informed at this point—not even the boys' families. The boys themselves would be held until further notice and excuses would be made shortly. Perhaps a government spokesmen would say they had been hired as live-in White House entertainers.

For now, however, the two were left to sit and think. Darren wondered how his mother would react to the news of him and Jamie being responsible for the greatest political catastrophe in the history of mankind. For starters, he'd be grounded, and right now, the idea of being safe and sound in his old, cramped bedroom seemed like the best of all possible worlds. When the thought of getting back his job at Jimmy Giraffe's sounded appealing as well, he realized he'd hit rock bottom.

Jamie had other concerns. "Darren."

"Huh?"

"They're gonna open our brains, aren't they?"

"What?"

"I saw it in a movie. A guy could kill people with his mind, and they opened his brain to find out how he did it."

"What did they find out?"

"He had an invisible ray in his head that rotted people's innards."

"Oh. Well, they're not going to open our brains, man."

"Why not?"

"Because! We can't even pull a rabbit out of a hat, much less rot people's *innards.*"

"We turned the President into a guinea pig! That's not normal!"

"Yeah, well, *you're* the one who turned him into a guinea pig," accused Darren. "Let's not start with this *we* business."

"*What?* You're gonna pin this on me alone? Nuh-uh, no way, dude!"

"Oh, oh, am *I* the one who rubbed the bottle and talked to the freak? I don't think so!"

"Yeah, but who made us walk *away* from the freak? We could have that bottle right now!"

"All right, all right," said Darren, caving, "but . . . Wait, that's it!"

"What?"

"We've just got to find the bottle, and *I'll* rub it this time! We'll turn everything back the way it was before, we'll make 'em forget about the guinea pig thing, and we'll still be the world's greatest magicians!"

"But we already looked for the bottle, and it wasn't there."

"Yeah, but we didn't look very hard. I'll bet it's still in that thrift shop. I just *know* it is."

There was a knock at the door, and, without awaiting a response, four FBI men entered with an overweight, serious-looking woman. She seemed like the kind of person who hadn't smiled or shown a hint of emotion, perhaps ever. Her brown hair was wrapped in a tight bun, and a large gold pentagonal pendant hung around her neck. She sized up the boys.

"Yeah, I've seen their act," she said in a low monotone voice. "Not bad."

"Not bad?" sniffed Jamie.

"Quiet," said Darren. "Hi."

"Hi, I'm Special Agent Joan Stonewell. My field is psychic phenomena, witchcraft, mythology, UFOs—basically anything that can't be explained by logic or science."

"Really?" said Jamie. "Hey, how come Superman wears his underpants outside of his tights?"

Stonewell remained expressionless. "Not my department. I heard you have a story to tell."

"You might say that," said Darren. "Where do you want us to start?"

"Try the beginning. You wanted to be magicians."

"Yeah," said Darren.

He and Jamie laid out the entire story for her, moment-by-moment, piece-by-piece. She seemed especially interested in details about the genie, though she remained silent throughout.

". . . and then his powers were gone and the President was still a guinea pig. And, uh, that's how we ended up here," finished Darren.

"You see?" added Jamie. "There's nothing wrong with my brain! Normal brain like everybody else! Nothing to see there, I can tell you that much!"

"Of that, I'm quite certain," said Stonewell blankly. "Thank you for your help. We'll be in touch." She headed for the door.

"You'll be in touch? What are we supposed to do until then?" asked Darren.

"Very little," she replied, and she left, followed by the FBI. The boys were alone once again.

"Very little?" said Jamie, thinking it through. "How will we know when we're done?"

Darren's head dropped back into his hands.

AGENT STONEWELL made a few quick phone calls, then ordered a top-secret meeting of the Vice President, the Chief of Staff, the Security Chief, the Press Secretary, and five other high-level staff members and aides. The guinea pig, now housed in a common pet's cage, was brought into the conference room. The assemblage sat around a long mahogany table.

The news was not good. Stonewell acknowledged that the boys' explanation, while indeed incredible, was also true. She told the story of the unseen entity that spawned the genie fable.

"It's been authenticated on at least three occasions," she said. "There is no actual genie, per se, like you see in the movies. In fact, it's officially known as a 'jinn,' a wandering spirit. Suffice to say, it's some sort of intelligent force which requires a host in order to appear in the flesh."

"What sort of host?" asked the Vice President.

"Any live being. Once it's summoned, it takes the form of a clear plasma which channels itself through whoever is nearby."

"But that's . . . simply impossible," insisted the Chief of Staff. Others grunted in agreement.

"It's not only possible, it's very real," she continued. "It was first documented in the Dead Sea Scrolls in the First Century A.D. The scrolls were lost, probably hidden by someone who had the bottle and didn't want it found. They were discovered in 1958, but the section about the bottle was spotted in a separate location, not far from the rest. That part was quickly discounted as, well, fanciful musings and almost discarded forever. Luckily, one of our first operatives rescued it from oblivion, and it's included in the classified National Archives here in D.C."

"But how could a thing like that exist?" asked an aide. "Where would it come from?"

Stonewell drew a deep breath, knowing this part would be

the most difficult for the assemblage to accept. "The force is an alien entity that got trapped on Earth somehow. The boys *and* the files concur that it was from another galaxy called Calysto ("Ridiculous," muttered the Security Chief, Howard Tyler), and the writings make it clear that there was some sort of virtual spaceship involved. Real, yet . . . not made of solid materials, at least ones that we know of. That's it."

"Oh, a magic genie in a ghooostly spaceship," mocked Tyler. Howard Tyler was a tall, gray-haired man of sixty-three with a square jaw and a straight, pointy nose. "Of course! Let's alert the Cartoon Network—they'll build a new show around it!"

"But we've never heard of this thing," said the Vice President, keeping a cooler head. "Who's had it before? Who's used it?"

"Have you ever heard of a man named Moses?" asked Agent Stonewell. A stunned silence followed. "He was one of the first, if not *thee* first. He couldn't get the pharaoh to free his people, but then he found the bottle, or perhaps the bottle found him. He used it to create the plagues, which he continued until his point was well taken. But after the slaves were freed, the pharaoh found out about this . . . magic receptacle. That's why he changed his mind and went after them."

"He . . . He just wanted the bottle," uttered the astounded Vice President.

Stonewell nodded. "Unfortunately for the pharaoh and his army, Moses still had the power, and, well, he apparently put it to good use."

"The parting of the Red Sea . . ." trailed the Vice President. "It was all true."

"But how could the bottle have ended up in a Salvation Army Thrift Shop, Agent Stonewell?" pressed Tyler.

"That I can't tell you. Chance. Fate. The bottle might have been passed along for decades or centuries at a time before anyone actually rubbed it, summoning the force. The bottom line, however, is that I am one hundred percent certain those boys are telling the truth. The President of the United States, ladies and gentlemen, is, in fact, that guinea pig."

All heads turned and stared at the animal. It was hopping around the cage in fits and starts, as if searching for an exit. The floor covering of cedar shavings tossed about.

"This is right when he'd normally be out on his afternoon jog," said another aide, gazing at the cage in awe.

"Looks like he's sticking to his schedule," said the Vice President. "So what do we do, Agent Stonewell? How should we proceed?"

"I don't know what you'll tell the public," said Stonewell, "but I do know that the bottle is out there somewhere, and that our only hope is to find it. There is something else, too. Something very important."

"What?" several asked in unison.

"His brain is one one-hundredth of the size it was before. He can't communicate with us, but he still has a basic awareness of what's going on around him. So, it is of the utmost importance for his sanity that he's treated as if he is still the President—at all times."

"You mean . . . he should stay in the Oval Office?" intoned Security Chief Tyler.

"Yes," confirmed Stonewell.

"What about all his meetings and conferences?" asked an aide.

"His schedule must not change," replied Stonewell. "He needs to be wherever he'd be if he were still . . . human. And the First Lady should be informed at once. Hopefully, she won't mind having a small creature flittering around the house."

Tyler could no longer handle it. "This is crazy!" he snapped. "I can't go on with this—it's completely nuts! It's *insane!* We're supposed to believe that President Brady is actually a—"

"Shhhhhhhhhhh!" they all scolded, looking back at the cage. The guinea pig was clawing and biting the thin metal bars.

"You've upset him!" said the Press Secretary in a loud whisper.

"Somebody should take him out of the cage," urged an aide.

After a moment, the Vice President stepped forward. He opened the lid, reached inside, and gingerly grasped the President of the United States around his teeny four-inch waist.

DARREN paced around the dining room, growing increasingly agitated. "Man, how are we going to get that bottle if we're locked in here?"

"Yeah, and how am I going to get to a bathroom? I gotta go bad."

"Ask one of the guards. Maybe they'll give you an *escort*."

Indeed, two armed guards were stationed outside the door, and one of them followed Jamie down the hall to a men's room. Once Jamie was settled in a stall, two of the President's aides entered. They spoke in whispers, which Jamie could overhear.

"I still can't believe how a thing like that is possible," said one.

"Well, there are just some things that can't be explained. We just have to accept what we see."

"That's for sure. Can you imagine what'll happen when the FBI finds that bottle? We'll be able to do *anything*. We'll have absolute power over the entire world!"

"It's too scary to even think about."

"What's so scary about being able to wipe out any enemy with a single wish?"

"It's true. We'll have the entire planet crawling at our feet."

Jamie held his breath as the men continued the discussion. Then, as they were washing their hands: "But what about those two boys? Won't they tell everyone what's going on?"

"Oh, don't worry about them. There are always methods of handling helpful people who now know . . . too much."

Jamie, peering through a crack in the door, watched as the man made a neck-slicing gesture with his hand. The other nodded as they exited the bathroom. A frightened Jamie let out a panicked yelp.

JAMIE burst back into the dining room and told Darren what he'd overheard. "They're going to kill us!" he concluded.

"See, I *told* you they didn't care about our brains," said Darren. "We've got to get out of here."

"Yeah, but how do we get past those two guards?"

The boys looked around and set their sights on a large air vent in the ceiling. Darren checked out a pair of draped red tablecloths and white window curtains. Maroon sashes dressed the high frames.

"Let's get to work," said Darren. Jamie dragged a table underneath the air vent as Darren yanked the curtains off their rods.

CHAPTER 15

Lindsay Cranford

WHILE THE BOYS planned their escape, things took a turn for the weird in the President's Oval Office. Security Chief Tyler, the Vice President, Agent Stonewell, the Press Secretary, and a few aides stood watching the stiff, brunette, no-nonsense First Lady, Margaret Brady, observe her husband as he sniffed a piece of cheese on his desk. Their attempt at explaining the situation to her had not gone at all well, and a painful tension filled the room.

"Hey, there. . . . Hey. . . . Hey, you, you, hey," she said, checking for any sign of recognition. "This is ridiculous," she snipped. "It doesn't know me. It's just a stupid animal."

"It *is* your husband, Mrs. Brady," explained Stonewell, "but his cognitive powers are, for the moment, the same as a guinea pig's. He picks up on subtle body language, so your nervousness *can* make him jittery and unresponsive. It might work better if you relaxed and spoke softly to him."

The First Lady looked at Stonewell as if the agent had just beamed in from Mars, but, seeing a roomful of anxious, concerned faces, she leaned forward and tried again.

"Honey? . . . Sweetheart? . . . Momma's Little Piggy Pi—" She sprang back up, more agitated. "Look, this is too ridiculous to even imagine. It *must* be some kind of a joke. Things like this just don't happen by themselves. I mean they don't happen at all!"

"I'm afraid it's not a joke, Margaret," tried the Vice President. "We wanted to exhaust *every* other possibility before we told you about this. We understand how . . . upsetting this has to be for you."

"Upsetting?" she snapped. *"Upsetting?* You're telling me that a pair of teenagers turned my husband into a vile, disgusting creature, and all you can say is that I might find this *upsetting?"*

"Margaret . . . " said the Vice President, worried that her outburst might upset the President.

"What?" she shot back at him. He opened his mouth to speak, then thought better of it. Her temper boiled over. "If this is some sort of wild put-on, I suggest you put an end to it *right now!"* she roared. "I never was and never will be game for the kind of infantile pranks my husband is likely to pull! And if *he* put you up to it, he'll remain President, but *your* heads are going to roll, *I swear to God!* Now, I will give you two seconds to tell me who is behind this *asinine farce!"* Her mouth quivered with rage. A stony silence ensued as no one

relished being the next to speak. The First Lady examined each face in the room, searching for a telling grin or a bead of sweat. That none were forthcoming only made her jaw tighten. "Oh!" she grunted in frustration.

She looked at the guinea pig, which stood on its hind legs, sniffing in her direction. It made a quiet chirping sound, and she peered at it pensively. *Could it be him?* She gave her head a solid shake, dismissing the thought.

DARREN struggled to shimmy through the narrow air vent they'd climbed into while Jamie lagged behind him. The speed of their journey was severely hampered by the crude costumes they wore, torn and tied from tablecloths and curtain sashes from the room.

"Come on!" admonished Darren. "We've got to get through here before they realize we're gone!"

"Oh, this'll never work, Darren. We don't look *anything* like dining tables."

"We're not dining tables, man! We're Arab sheiks!"

"Oh, yeah, yeah, okay."

They reached an opening at the other end, and Darren gingerly removed the vent cover. He peered out into a hallway, at ankle level. When the coast was clear, he motioned for Jamie to follow. They squeezed out of the vent and fixed their outfits. Red cloth napkins were wrapped around their heads like turbans, and the gold curtain sashes held the tablecloths around their bodies.

They turned a corner and found themselves in a busy hallway, with scores of people scurrying back and forth. The boys were able to walk among them, almost unnoticed. At the end of the hallway, however, they spotted a Secret Service woman with a headset, carefully observing the crowd. They turned in the opposite direction and saw a man in a similar outfit. They were stuck.

Fortunately, another White House tour group was passing through. The boys quickly joined them, trying to blend into their ranks. It worked—they passed the Secret Service man, then took off down a stairwell and snuck out of the building.

AT THE SAME TIME, the Salvation Army Thrift Shop in downtown Washington was in for a shock to its system. It was a Tuesday, their weekly *Half-Off For Seniors Day.* Lindsay, the freckle-nosed employee, had just left.

A swarm of FBI cars pulled up in front, slammed on their brakes, and dashed out. Twenty agents in dark suits bolted into the store at once. Frightened seniors scampered out as the manager, a paunchy, bespectacled man in a brown tweed jacket, rushed to the front. Before he could speak, an agent flashed his badge and said, "FBI. We need to find something." The agent handed the manager a check. "I think this should cover everything."

The manager eyed the sum and his mouth popped open. "Yes! Yes, take anything you want! Or everything! Thank you, thank you!" Some of the agents were already at work, overturning boxes of clothing and toys.

"Thought that might do it," said the agent. He turned to a wooden case with shelves of glassware and knick-knacks. He picked up a vase from the top shelf, gave it a look, and tossed it on the floor, shattering it. With a swipe of his hand, he added the contents of the rest of the shelf.

Quickly, the room was teeming with male and female agents, searching and destroying racks of items. The manager, both thrilled and nervous, asked the FBI man, "Excuse me, uh, what exactly are you all looking for?"

"A magic bottle."

"Oh!" said the manager, as if understanding. Getting into the game, he swept a row of ceramic bowls off a shelf. He was going to thoroughly enjoy this.

DARREN AND JAMIE, still in their sheik outfits, exited to the street and tried to wave down a taxi.

"Hey! Hey, stop!" they pleaded. Several taxis sped by, ignoring them.

One old powder-blue car, however, passed by, screeched to a halt, hit reverse, and stopped in front of them. It was a Plymouth Fury III from the 60s, with one long front seat. The boys looked in—it was Lindsay. Her small dog, a Chihuahua, sat next to her.

"Hey, it's you, from the thrift shop!" said Jamie.

"Good call," said Lindsay. "What, did Halloween come early this year?"

"It's a long story. Can we get a ride?" Darren pleaded.

"Sure, why not," said Lindsay. "I love long stories. And this one's gotta be trippy. Scoot over, Hambone." The dog scampered next to her as the boys hopped in—Darren in front, Jamie in back. She drove off. "I thought you guys were kidding when you said you were magicians, and now you're, like, the most famous ones in the world."

"Thanks," said Darren. "We, uh, just worked hard at it."

"I guess. You're pretty incredible. But what's with the outfits?"

"Oh, this stuff?" said Darren. "Nothing, really. Just out having some fun. Nothing odd about it at—cops!"

A police car passed slowly on the right. Lindsay watched both of her charges shield their faces, and she shook her head. "Yeah, just two world-famous magicians hanging outside the White House, on the run from the law while wearing lacy tablecloths," she quipped. "Nothing odd there."

"Uh, well, it's a long story," repeated Darren.

"So you said."

"Uh, listen, would you mind driving us back to your store?" asked Darren. "There's something else there we could use."

"Oh, like salt and pepper shakers for the tablecloths?" joked Lindsay. "You could be a whole Italian diner."

Jamie laughed uproariously. "Ha, ha, haaaaaaa! That's really good! You hear that, Darren?" he said, slapping the back of his shoulder. "We could be a whole Italian diner!"

"Yeah, yeah, I was right here, man."

"All right, we'll go," sighed Lindsay, "but I just came from there. It's been a long week. We had to go through everything and get rid of stuff."

"Get rid of stuff?" squeaked Darren. "What kind of stuff did you get rid of?"

"Ah, just stuff that nobody bought in the last year or two."

The boys exchanged a worried look. Jamie said, "If a thrift shop doesn't want something anymore, do they give it to another thrift shop?"

"No, silly, they throw it in the garbage."

"Oh, my God!" exclaimed Darren.

Lindsay scrunched her forehead. "Has this got something to do with the long story you guys have?"

"What would make you think that?" asked Darren. "Now could you, uh, step on it please, Lindsay? We've got to get there really fast!"

Lindsay came to an intersection and made a right turn.

Darren panicked. "Hey, isn't the store off to the left?"

"Yes, but I thought we might take the scenic route."

"*Why?*"

"You have a long story to tell me. Wouldn't want you to have to cut it short." She gave Darren a sly smile.

"Okay, turn around and we'll tell you the whole thing," said Darren. "Please!"

"Okee-dokey," she said. "Hold on to my dog for a second."

"Why?" said Darren, picking up Hambone.

Lindsay, a daredevil driver, spun the wheel hard. The tires screeched, and the car whipped around in the road, making a complete U-turn.

"*Aaaaaaaaaaaaah!*" the boys shouted, trying to hang on.

The turn completed, Lindsay smiled and drove toward the thrift shop.

"My dad was a race car driver," she said. "Taught me a few little tricks. Okay, so I'm ready for that story. Spill."

The boys just looked at her, their faces ashen white.

THE TWO White House aides, whom Jamie had seen in the men's room, plus two large, tough-looking men in black turtlenecks, strode toward the room where the boys had been held.

"Has the Vice President okayed the, uh, procedure?" whispered one aide to the other.

"Well, sort of. He said to get rid of them."

"Are you sure he didn't mean to just let them go?"

"If he meant that, he would have *said* that, wouldn't he?"

"Maybe, but shouldn't we, uh, check to make sure that—"

"These gentlemen have handled these situations before," said the aide, referring to the men in black. "I think they know what the Vice President meant." The men's cold looks left little doubt as to the goal of their mission.

The armed guards at the door let the four men in. They quickly realized the boys were gone.

"They . . . They've escaped!" the first aide exclaimed.

"This is not good," said the other.

The disappointed tough-looking men turned and glared at the aides, causing them to shudder.

LINDSAY'S PLYMOUTH neared the thrift shop as Darren finished a speedy retelling of their adventure. ". . . and then you picked us up and here we are," he concluded.

"Huh," said Lindsay.

"Do you believe me?"

"No, but it's a fun story. You should make that part of your next TV special."

"But it's true!" insisted Darren. "There's no next special if we don't find the bottle!"

"The government wants to steal our powers and take over the world!" added Jamie.

"Well, maybe you could bargain with them," joked Lindsay. "You get one half of the world, they get the other. Get Hawaii up front, though. Tell them it's just not part of the deal."

"*What?*" said Darren, thoroughly annoyed. "Just let us out. We've gotta go find that bottle before . . . "

They reached the shop and realized with horror that they were entirely too late. Lindsay slowed the car, and her mouth fell open as they surveyed the scene of destruction behind the windows. No one was present except a few passersby who peered inside.

"What in the world?" said Lindsay. "I was just here! What happened?"

"They beat us to it," said Darren sadly.

"Yeah," agreed Jamie. "Look at that."

"What? Who beat you to it?" said Lindsay.

"The FBI, probably," said Darren.

"Yeah, right," sniffed Lindsay, her eyes rolling in their sockets. "Where is everybody? I'm calling the police!" She grabbed her cell phone.

"Forget it," said Darren. "They already know about it."

"So why aren't they here yet?" challenged Lindsay.

"Oh, man, nothing can save us now," said Jamie. "We're just sittin' ducks, ready for slaughter."

"Because somebody robbed the place?" said Lindsay, totally confused.

"Don't you get it?" said Darren, erupting. "I was telling you the truth! They came looking for the bottle before we did!"

"Looks like they got it," said Jamie.

"Gee, ya think?" piped Darren.

Jamie heaved a worried sigh. "What do we do now?"

"Let's go to your mom's house," said Darren. "They're probably already looking for us at ours."

DARREN WAS RIGHT. Inga was beside herself, trying to stop the FBI from destroying every last item in the mansion.

"Doze boys are real mageek, so you batter wadj out! Dey'll turn you eentoo a bonch of sneks, becozz thad's whot you are!"

The army of agents ignored her as they overturned shelves, tore open pillows, and searched every nook and cranny in pursuit of the bottle.

Finally, Inga couldn't take it anymore. She packed her bags

and stormed out, saying, "Tell dose boys I hed enoff! If dey vant me, I'll bih dancink in de finest nightclob effer beelt near an airport!"

She slammed the door behind her.

LINDSAY DROVE THE BOYS to the Jenks' household and gave Darren her cell phone number on a slip of paper.

"If you ever need to be saved from any evil FBI men, don't hesitate to call," she said, playfully mocking them. The boys thanked her and left.

She drove back to her small studio apartment where she opened a can of dog food while checking her phone messages. There were two calls from friends, one from her mother, and one from her boss—"We won't need you tomorrow, Lindsay," he said, oddly upbeat. "You might not believe this, but the place was destroyed by the FBI just about an hour ago." Lindsay gasped and dropped the dog food can. "They came in and ransacked the place looking for a some kind of a magic bottle, they said. Can you believe that? Crazy stuff! They paid for it all, though. And don't worry—we'll be up and running again in a few days, and I'll call you when I need you back. Bye for now."

Lindsay couldn't believe her ears. *Darren's tale was true? That bizarre, dopey story?* Hambone, in the meantime, hungrily attacked the fallen food.

"Hambone! Don't eat off the floor!"

She scooped the rest of the food back into the can, then grabbed a roll of paper towels from over the sink. The towel holder sat next to a bottle with two scrub brushes sticking out of it. She wet a few towels, walked toward the leftover mess on the floor, and—

She stopped dead in her tracks.

She turned and looked at the bottle with the brushes, which she had pulled from the thrift shop garbage bin a few days before. But it was just an old piece of junk, she thought; weird looking, like a prop from a cheap sci-fi show, which was actually why she liked it. Not even a top to it. Could it be . . . ?

She removed the brushes, then gingerly picked up the bottle and examined it. She turned it upside down—nothing came out. She peered inside—nothing to see. She studied its strange markings and suddenly felt very silly.

"No magic genie here," she mumbled to herself.

She fumbled with the bottle and it fell into a dirty pot, soaking in the sink.

"Oh, good move," she muttered, and she grabbed the bottle and rinsed it off. She wiped it with a rag, rubbing it back and forth until dry.

"There you go, Mr. Genie," she joked, and she stood the bottle up and replaced the brushes. She knelt down to pet Hambone, who happily devoured the rest of his dinner.

Suddenly, a clear undulating gas cloud oozed from the bottle, slowly floating toward Lindsay's back. As she stood, the cloud vanished. Lindsay rinsed the dog food can and threw it into a bag of recyclables. Seeing that the bin was full, she tied the bag and took it out to the hallway.

The moment she left, the bubble reappeared behind Hambone, shrank to his size, and *fwoosh*—it flew right at him, disappearing into his body. Hambone froze. His body stiffened and his eyes opened wide.

Lindsay returned and washed her hands. "Time for *me* to eat something, Hambone."

"Hello," replied a voice, clear as day.

"*Aaaaaaah!*" shrieked Lindsay, startled. She spun around, her face filled with abject terror. "Who is it? Who's there?" she yelled, and she yanked the pan out of the sink, the water and suds sloshing about. She grasped the pan's handle with both hands and wielded it threateningly. "*Where are you, who was that?*"

Her back slammed into a corner, causing a wave of water to splash from the pan. Hambone calmly looked up at her and said, "I am Zoltrad from the Calysto Galaxy. I am commonly known as a genie. You have three wishes."

Lindsay stared at her dog, then issued a bloodcurdling scream.

IN JAMIE'S BASEMENT, Darren busily strung wads of wires together, which all connected to a black transformer box he had grabbed from Jamie's old train set.

"When will your mom be back?" asked Darren.

"Around five."

"Good. I figure we've got a few hours before the FBI even

thinks to look for us here. And if they found the bottle, maybe they'll forget about us anyway."

"Yeah. But what's the plan for if they *don't* forget about us?"

"Well, outside of what I'm doing now, the plan, as far as I can see it is"—he thought hard—"to come up with a plan."

"Oh, man, there's no plan!" moaned Jamie, collapsing on the floor.

"Relax, man. Ainsley will be here soon and then we'll figure out what to do next, okay?"

"Oh, why didn't we listen to my mother and just work on getting into college?" cried Jamie. "We had to become all rich and famous and have the FBI after us." A thought struck him, and he sat up. "Hey, Darren. How come on TV, the FBI is always the good guys?"

"Because it's TV, man. Now help me out here. I need you to hold the pliers."

They heard *banging* from upstairs, and they froze.

"It's them!" said Darren.

"It could be my mom," said Jamie. They listened further to the increasingly heavy, violent pounding.

Darren whispered, "Does your mother use a battering ram to get into the house?"

"No, but my daddy did once."

They heard the front door busting open and a voice yelling, "You guys go upstairs. We'll check the basement!"—followed by stomping feet.

Darren pulled a lever on the transformer box while Jamie

grabbed Maxwell, and they raced to the back of the room. They switched off the light, climbed three stairs, and exited through a pair of swinging doors that led to the backyard.

Instantly, the basement door flung open, and seven dark-suited FBI men raced down, guns drawn. A sweaty, thin-faced man in front—their captain—saw the back doors slam shut. "There they go!" he said.

They sprinted toward the back. The first stage of Darren's plan worked—the captain's foot tripped a wire, which activated the transformer. The wires led to the eighteen Super Sucker brooms, all lined up in three rows. The entire fleet suddenly sprang to life, headlights blazing and motors roaring. They advanced on the men like a mechanical militia. The men stopped short, amazed.

"What the hell are those?" shouted one.

"Who cares?" said the captain. "Come on, those kids are getting away!"

They tried running to the back, but had no idea what formidable opponents they had in the blazing brooms. The first broom swung wayward and tripped one of the men. "Bwaaaaaaaa!" he yelled as he flew onto his face. Three other men piled on top of him with a round of "Hey's!" and "Oof's!"

Another machine attacked the captain's legs, exactly the way the first broom had attacked Jamie's boss. "Aaaaaahhhhh!" he yelled. "Get it off of me! *Get it ooooff!*"

The machine knocked him over, and he was out-matched by the onslaught of churning wheels and spinning broom heads. Two other men tried to free him, but the heavy machine sputtered and sparked, shocking them. They cried out and staggered backwards. Other machines descended upon them, quickly taking them down.

Two of the men from upstairs, hearing the commotion, ran down and tried tackling the machines. One man leapt onto a broom, knocking it over with a *crash,* but the machine, completely intact, seemed to wrestle him, its broom heads deftly pinning him to the ground. "Yaaaaaaaahhh!" he screamed as the wheels climbed onto his shoulders, rendering him helpless.

The last three men ran down and looked about in horror at the dismal, deafening, dust-filled display. Five machines which, at first, had wandered astray, instantly attacked them from behind. The surprised men succumbed quickly to the mechanical marauders, yelling and fighting futilely to free themselves.

A large muscular man locked his arm around a machine's handle, and, grunting and grimacing, he took it to the floor and beat it with his fist. Another man, chased by two other machines, tripped on top of him. The Super Suckers made quick work of them both, surrounding and vanquishing them in a blaze of sputtering sparks and billowing smoke. A tangle of flailing arms and legs protruded from the machines.

The captain managed to escape his attacker, and, mangled but determined, he neared the back doors. Two machines lurched toward him, and he aimed his gun and snarled,

"Eat this, you overgrown tricycles!" He unleashed a round of gunfire, which only seemed to anger the brooms. Their motors let out a *bang,* which kicked them into to a higher, ear-piercing gear. They plowed forward at the frightened man, who backed into two other machines. He fell down and disappeared between the four of them. They closed in, chomping down and burning rubber.

It was grim sight, the likes of which had never been seen before and would, most likely, never be seen again.

CHAPTER 16

Princess Lindsay

DARREN AND JAMIE, unaware of the military victory behind them, ran as fast as they could down residential streets. A car drove up to them, honking. The boys had never been so happy to see Ainsley Grosspucker.

"Guys, hey!" he said.

The boys jumped in and a nervous Ainsley drove off. "What was going on back there?" he asked suspiciously. "There were five cars at the house, and no one answered the door."

"Uh, well," said Darren, trying to dream up a good story. "You see, the—"

"The FBI was trying to kill us!" yelled Jamie.

Darren sighed and closed his eyes, again annoyed by his best friend's habit of blabbing everything.

"The FBI, huh?" said Ainsley. "Okay, I know exactly what's going on here. You don't have to say another word."

"You know?" asked a surprised Darren.

"Sure," said Ainsley. "I have eyes. I'm not dumb."

"When did you catch on?" asked Jamie.

"I've known it all along. In fact, I've been *expecting* this. The *FBI?* I at least deserve a better excuse, you, you two-timing backstabbers!"

The boys exchanged an incredulous look.

"What are you talking about, Ainsley?" asked Jamie.

"You're leaving me and joining a bigger talent agency! Anyone can see that! Why else would you run when you saw me coming?"

"No, Ainsley," said Darren. "There are no other agents. At least not the talent kind."

"Oh, no? Then whose cars were those, really?"

The boys exchanged another look. Darren took a breath and told Ainsley the whole story, sparing no details. Ainsley, unlike Lindsay, believed it immediately. After all, the boys did all their shows without preparation or rehearsals, including making the Leaning Tower of Pisa stand straight as a flagpole. He knew something bizarre was going on—possibly even supernatural—but as far as he was concerned, it didn't matter. He represented the greatest act in the world, and questioning it could only lead to trouble. But now, *the President of the United States was a guinea pig? And the FBI was after the boys?* This was a good deal more than he could handle.

Darren finished the story. " . . . and so you see, we need you, Ainsley. You've got to help us find a way out of this mess!"

"Okay, okay, let me think—I've just got to figure out what's the best thing to do. Okay, I've got it." Ainsley slammed on his brakes, causing all to lurch forward. A car behind them honked angrily and screeched by.

"What are you doing?" said Darren.

"You have to get out," said Ainsley.

"What?" they yelped.

"Get out! I can't save you from the FBI! If you stay here, they'll get me, too!" He nervously checked his rearview mirror. "You're on your own!"

The boys looked at each other, unsure.

"*Get out of here right now!*" Ainsley bellowed, scared out of his mind.

The shocked duo jumped out of the car, and Ainsley sped off, the open doors flapping. Darren and Jamie stood on the sidewalk, dumbstruck.

"That was so wrong," said Darren.

"Ice cold," agreed Jamie. "That's our agent."

"Not anymore. Now he's just a wacked weasel."

"What do we do now?"

"I don't know."

"Hey, what about Lindsay?" said Jamie.

"What about her?"

"Her number's in your pocket. Maybe she can help us."

Darren stared at him, impressed. "That is a really good idea."

"Duh!" replied Jamie. "Call her!"

Darren grabbed his cell phone and dug out Lindsay's number.

MEANWHILE, in the year 847 A.D., in a medieval Arabian castle, Princess Lindsay was comfortably splayed out on an ornate Corinthian couch on a golden marble platform. She wore a lacy silver and sky-blue sequined dress and a diamond tiara, which encircled her head like a sparkling halo. Every part of her body dripped with ruby, diamond, and emerald jewelry. She was very content, having her every whim catered to by a team of eight strapping men in togas. One played a harp, and another, a flute. Two performed interpretive dances as others fanned her with giant palm leaves. Another man stood over her, feeding her grapes and strawberries.

Nearby, Hambone, back to his normal canine self, sat on a very small throne and dined on bacon, ham hocks, and biscuits. A gold lamé bib caught the spillover.

"Lovely! Looooovely, fellows!" said Lindsay grandly. "Fill me with the nectar of the earth, and entertain me, you maaaarvelous servants. I will allow you to adore me as long as you shall live. More, please, mooore!"

It hadn't taken her long to calm down and warm to Zoltrad's offer. Her first wish, to be a real Arabian princess in ancient times, came true immediately, and she was relishing every second.

Suddenly, the nursery rhyme, "Do Your Ears Hang Low?" pierced the air with an electronic twang. Lindsay looked around, puzzled and annoyed.

"What is that? Where is that infernal noise coming—Oh, drat!" She reached into the folds of her dress and produced her cell phone, which squeaked the offending music. "I knew

I should have left this home." She answered it. "If this isn't the King of Siam, I really have to bolt."

"Uh, Lindsay?" said Darren, in another time and place entirely.

"That would be *Princess* Lindsay to you, whoever you are," she said while examining her tinkly diamond bracelet.

"It's Darren," he said, wondering why she sounded so strange.

"Darren, Darren," she drawled, apparently unable to place him.

"Yes. Remember, you picked us up in your car? . . . Today?"

"Oh, Daaaaaarren, yes. I do recall you now. How are you and your little friend doing?"

Darren looked incredulously at the phone. (Jamie mouthed "*What?*") He got back on. "Not great at the moment, uh, *Princess*. We were wondering if you could help us out."

"I *am* a little tied up at the moment, actually," she said, her mouth stuffed with grapes.

"I can't quite hear you, but listen, this is a matter of life and death! The FBI is after us! We're at Connecticut Avenue and Seventeenth, and we really need you to come and get us right now!"

"Well, I'd love to, but I'm not really *here,* per se."

"What? Where are you?"

"Somewhere near Egypt, I'm told, but frankly, I don't think we've conquered the whole area yet. The entire West Nile is still up for grabs."

"Uh . . . are you okay?"

"Oh, I'm better than I have ever been, and I plan to get better and better!" She let out a hearty laugh. "Ta-ta, my friend."

She clicked off her phone and addressed the servants. "Now, how in the world did they reach me when I'm thousands of years in the past? Ucch, must be that new anytime-minutes calling plan. Remind me to cancel it. Oh, better yet," she said, handed the phone to one of the men, "just destroy this thing, won't you, Augustus?"

The man took the phone and left the room. She then reflected for a moment. "Hmm, my little friends are in some sort of trouble. . . . Well, I'm sure they'll be fine. More grapes!"

A servant complied.

"WHAT HAPPENED? Is she coming?" Jamie asked hopefully.

"No. She was all weird sounding. And she wanted me to call her Princess Lindsay."

"Princess Lindsay?"

"Yeah, can you believe that?"

"Wow," said Jamie dreamily. "All that time we spent with her, and we didn't even know she was a princess."

"What? She's *not* a princess, moron! She works in a thrift shop!"

"Maybe she's undercover, observing the common folk. I saw it in a movie once."

Darren smacked him on the back of his head.

"Ow!" said Jamie. "What did you do that for?"

"There was no other way to say it."

Jamie spotted a police car heading their way. "Cops!"

The two turned, dropped their heads, and continued on down the sidewalk, ducking behind a few passersby. The police car drove past them.

"Close call," said Darren. "Come on, we'll go to the thrift shop. I'm guessing someone grabbed that thing before the FBI got there, but they might have records of who bought what. We'll track that thing down if it's the last thing we do."

Jamie shook his head. "Well, if we don't find it, it'll *definitely* be the last thing we do."

They passed an electronics store just as a news show was airing on a TV set in the window. The anchorman said, "—and no one seems to know the current whereabouts of President Brady."

"Hey!" said Darren, and they stopped to listen.

The anchorman continued: "All of his meetings were cancelled again today, and the White House will only say that he is on some sort of special trip. Opponents are calling this a cheap ploy to stop a key tax bill from passing this week. In a decidedly lighter development, there's a new presidential pet—a guinea pig. White House officials are taking great pains to make the animal feel welcome."

The program showed Secret Service personnel jogging behind the guinea pig, which scurried about the back lawn of the White House.

"Here's a scene you don't see too often," said the anchorman, smiling. "The animal seems to be running circles around all the President's men. We'll be right back."

"You're right—we've got to find that bottle, and fast," said Darren, hurrying on down the sidewalk. "And we've got to stay calm so no one notices us, okay?"

"Yeah," said Jamie, catching up to him. "Stayin' calm."

They walked by a fancy Italian restaurant. Jamie peeked in and stopped short, sparking recognition.

"Darren, look. I think I know that guy from somewhere," he said, pointing.

"Who?"

"At the back table. The guy with the red tie."

Darren looked. Suddenly, his eyes and, in fact, his whole face, widened. He and Jamie recognized the man.

"The geniiiiie!" they shouted.

"Get him!" yelled Darren.

The customer from the thrift shop, who had been momentarily turned into the genie, was having a formal business dinner with his new clients—all Japanese men and women. He was a commercial realtor and was on the verge of a sixty million dollar sale. He pulled out a contract and a pen.

"Just sign on the line and the tower is yours," he said with a smile. His clients seemed pleased as they took the contract.

Just then, a commotion was heard at the front door. The clients turned and watched as two boys ran inside.

"Excuse me! Excuse me! Sorry!" the boys yelled.

The stuffy maitre d,' who wore a tuxedo and a bad hairpiece, was taken by surprise. "What, what are you—You can't run in here like that! Just one minute—*hey!*"

The boys bolted by him and past the formally dressed patrons, knocking into chairs and causing a stir in the room. Many customers, recognizing the boys, stood to get a better look. A waiter, holding a full food tray, lurched backward to avoid getting bumped into by the two; he just managed to keep his tray level. He turned to see what was happening and got rushed headlong by the maitre d', who was hurdling toward the boys. Both the maitre d' and the waiter went down with the *crash* and *clatter* of splayed-out entrees.

"Uh, this is, uh, nothing to worry about," said the ex-genie to his very concerned clients. "Just some local riff-raff. Nothing to be, uh . . ." The man then realized the boys were racing right toward him. "What the—"

"Heeeey!" yelled Jamie.

"What do you want?" said the man. "Who are you?"

"It's you!" shouted Darren. *"It's the genie!"*

"What? I'm *what?*"

"Genie, it's me! It's Jamie, the guy you talked to in the thrift shop!"

The clients eyed their host, anticipating his response.

"I'm sure I have no idea what you're talking about," declared the man.

"You, you have a daughter named Emily!" said Jamie, remembering the man's cell phone call. The Japanese clients nodded, having met his daughter.

The man was shocked. "Well, uh, yeah, but—"

"You were getting her a costume! She was crying!"

"Now, wha, how did you know that?" said the man, beginning to panic. "I have no idea how they knew that," he assured his clients. "This is the most ridiculous thing I have ever—"

"Those are magicians from television," one client chimed in.

"Oh, yes, they are very good," added another. The rest agreed, praising the duo.

"You told Jamie all about the three wishes!" continued Darren.

"Come on, you remember!" pleaded Jamie. "You told me to come with you, and I could have anything I wanted! Anything at all!"

"*What?*" said the man, leaping from his seat. "I certainly did not! I said nothing of the kind to anyone!"

"Oh, no, wait," said Darren. "Does somebody here own him now? Is he someone else's genie?"

The clients looked confused and upset. "Should we continue the meeting another time?" asked a female client.

"What? No!" boomed the man. "I have never seen these guys in my life! Isn't there somebody who can get these lunatics out of here?"

Indeed, the restaurant manager and a few burly cooks were striding toward the boys. They did not look happy.

Darren, seeing them approaching, grabbed the man's lapels. "No, wait, listen to me!" he ranted. "You started all this, genie!

You've got to fix it! *You've got to save us!*"

The manager and the cooks grabbed the boys from behind. Darren held on tightly to the man's jacket while they dragged Jamie, kicking and screaming, toward the front.

"We'll do anything for you, genie!" yelled Jamie. "Anything at all, we promise!"

"You are out of here right now, dipstick!" growled the manager.

"Give us more wishes, genie!" pleaded Darren, shaking the man. "We'll do whatever you say this time!"

"Let go of me, you insane idiot!" yelled the man.

His agitated clients conferred while a cook lifted Darren onto his shoulders and carried him out.

"Put me down! Put me down!" yelled Darren. "That's the genie! *That's hiiiim!*"

"No, *I'm* the genie, pal, and I'm makin' you disappear," snarled the cook.

"I'm very sorry, ladies and gentlemen," said the man to his clients. He fixed his collar, wiped his brow, and got back to business. "Now, where were—"

The clients all stood up. "Very sorry. Must go now," one said.

"But the deal!" said the man. "Just sign it and we're done!"

"You upset the famous and honorable men," explained a male client. "Something must be wrong with you . . . Jeanie."

"Jeanie? No, no, my name is Robert, just like I told you! They thought I was a, a, a *genie!*" he sputtered. "Not *Jeanie,* the name, but some kind of magical . . ." The clients pushed in their chairs, ignoring him. "I never asked them to do anything! I don't even know them! *Wait!*"

But it was all over—the clients exited. The man fell back into his chair, beaten and bewildered.

The cook and manager discarded the boys onto the sidewalk. "You can't do this! We're famous!" said Darren, not caring how pathetic he sounded.

"Well, then, I'm sure you'll enjoy signing autographs down at the police station," said the manager. "They'll be here any second."

"*The police?*" shouted Darren. "No, man, please, there's no need for police! We're sorry, we'll clean dishes, anything!"

Sirens blared in the distance. Passenger vehicles scurried toward the curb as fifteen police cars and motorcycles raced to the site. From the opposite direction, more sirens announced the appearance of enough speeding police cars to fill a city block. The manager and the cooks looked on, surprised at the size of the turnout.

"What the heck?" said the manager. "You guys must be in some real kind of trouble."

"Who, little old us?" said Darren. He looked at Jamie, and the two of them, hitting on the same idea, deftly slipped past the men and sprinted back into the restaurant.

"Hey!" shouted the manager. "Get 'em!" The cooks rushed back inside.

The boys, at a fever-pitch panic, barreled past the newly

alarmed patrons, running into chairs, knocking over flower arrangements and champagne buckets, and headed toward the kitchen doors in back. The maitre d' and the ex-genie tried to catch them, but were way too slow for the panicked duo.

The boys charged into the kitchen, raced past startled assistant cooks, and exited out the back.

The police poured into the restaurant, guns in the air, causing mass panic and hysteria. Tables, chairs, and waiters were upended as the terrified patrons screamed and rushed to the exit.

"There is no cause for alarm!" shouted the manager, drowned out by the din. "Please be seated! I'm very sorry! Dessert is on us! Dessert is on—"

A flying dessert tray hit him in the face, and he staggered backward and fell. The onrushing police stepped over him, eyes peeled for their prey.

THEIR PREY, in the meantime, sprinted down three blocks of back alleys. When they finally dared to peek behind them, they saw nothing and no one.

"I think . . . we're safe," said Darren, panting hard, his face full of sweat. His heavyset body was not made for running.

"Yeah," said Jamie.

"Let's . . . keep going," he managed.

"Yeah."

They resumed their getaway, but heard approaching sirens. Red lights flashed at the end of the alley, and a police car pulled up with a *screech,* blocking their path. The boys stopped short and yelled in fright as another car appeared, followed by three more. An officer shouted, "Stop! Police!" as others leapt from the vehicles.

Among them were Officers John Tierney and Margo Hellard. During their time off after the thrift shop incident, they vacationed together, fell in love, and were now engaged. They were shocked when they first saw the boys on TV, and, despite their months of therapy, they concluded that the magic duo did indeed have special powers. It was the only way they could explain the shop's broken and restored windows. They kept their feelings strictly between themselves, though—if they wanted to stay on the police force, no one could know what they really thought.

When they drew guns and saw the boys, they looked at each other, eyes widened. *It's them.* They looked on with a combination of exhilaration and fright.

The boys were too frantic to see them, however.

"Other way!" yelled Darren, and the two turned and ran.

Police Chief Belson exited from a car and strode over to the officers. Since the day of his embarrassing exposé in the newspaper, he'd embraced his adoration for Barney and had a large Barney cutout sewn to the back of his uniform. No one ever dared mention it.

"Nobody shoot!" he ordered in his usual gruff tone. "We'll be taking these guys in unharmed."

Jamie and Darren tore down the alley, but more police cars skidded to a halt at the other end, blocking them in. The boys stopped and looked about as scores of policemen knelt down, guns trained on them.

"This is the Chief of Police!" Belson boomed into a megaphone. "Stop right there! You're completely surrounded!"

Belson was right—they had no means of escape. There was an empty parking lot beside them, but it was completely brick-walled, with no back exit. From where the police were positioned, they couldn't see into the parking lot, but they knew the boys were trapped.

Darren and Jamie looked at each other, realizing it was time to give up. But then—

Flash!

A shocking ray of blinding light flooded the parking lot. Jamie and Darren shielded their eyes, and the police strained theirs to see what was happening. But only the boys witnessed an astounding sight—a lightning bolt struck the center of the lot with a *sonic boom,* and a car broke through it in a torrent of dust and smoke. It was Lindsay's Plymouth Fury III, with Lindsay behind the wheel. A bewildered Hambone rode in back, awkwardly strapped into a seatbelt. The car screeched to a halt.

"I think we know where the bottle went," said Darren.

"No doubt," agreed Jamie.

"Get in!" yelled Lindsay.

"There's police all over!" said Darren, dashing into the front seat and slamming the door. Jamie jumped in back.

"Oh, yeah? Fasten your seatbelts and watch my smoke."

She floored it and skidded into the alleyway, swinging the steering wheel.

"What in the world?" said Belson, lowering the megaphone.

"Let's move," whispered a worried Tierney to his fiancé, Hellard. "There's no telling what evil they'll conjure up this time." Hellard nodded, and the two retreated to a spot well behind the others.

Lindsay's car screeched and turned, and the back fender *slammed* into the brick wall. Inside, boys and dog alike were pinned back in their seats as the car headed right at the police vehicles. Lindsay's eyes were locked in a manic glare as she flew toward them. The policemen leapt aside, but Belson stood resolute.

"Stop! Halt!" he boomed into the megaphone.

"Don't hit that guy!" yelled Jamie.

"Hey, it's the Barney guy," said Darren, looking closer.

Jamie recognized the chief. "Oh, yeah! Hey, Barney guy!" he called out. "Super-dee-du-"

He wasn't able to finish the sentence. Lindsay steered away from Belson, and the Fury III *smashed* into the police cars. It busted through the barricade in a deluge of twisted metal and flying glass.

The boys yelled as Lindsay jerked the wheel and spun the car in the direction of the main road. The back wheels, squealing, jumped the curb and sped forward. The car zipped to the end of the block and twisted once again down the street.

She made it through a yellow light and turned onto a clear open road.

"After them!" ordered Belson. The officers jumped back into their dented, twisted cars, hit the sirens, and burned rubber.

"Wow!" exclaimed Darren, straightening himself up.

"Awesome!" declared Jamie, readjusting his shoulder strap.

"Oh, that was nothing," said Lindsay. "You should have seen me totally destroy the field at the Monster Car Rally in Philadelphia last year."

"Wish we could have been there," said Darren with a grimace. He grasped his neck, turning it side to side to ease a slight sprain.

"Why do they want us so badly?" said Jamie. "Just because we turned the President into a guinea pig?"

"I'd rate that a good guess," said Lindsay, keeping the gas pedal flush with the floor. The swarm of police was hot on her trail, motorcycles leading the way.

"They're gaining on us!" said Darren. "Can you go faster?"

"This car's a dinosaur. It's a miracle it can go anywhere."

Deep rumbling was heard overhead, and a spotlight hit the car. The boys peered out and saw a pair of police helicopters hovering above them.

"Oh, man, they brought out the choppers!" cried Darren. "We're finished! It's over!"

"Maybe not," said Lindsay.

Darren looked at the motorcycles, now just ten yards behind them, and hollered, "Well, if you've got an idea, you might want to try it sometime around now!"

"Oh man, you guys'll owe me big time," she said, and she muttered to herself. The only word the boys heard was "bubbles."

"Bubbles?" said Darren.

His confusion was quickly cleared up as, instantly, bubbles appeared from underneath the car—hundreds at first, then thousands, then tens of thousands. They ballooned out in every direction, floating toward the oncoming motorcycles. The officers had only enough time to blurt out, "What the . . ." before they were enveloped and blinded by the soapy orbs. A few motorcycles stopped short—those in back slammed into the others. All jumped from the seats and raced to the curb just in time—the multitudes of police cars behind them skidded into the bikes. Mass destruction followed as the entire fleet, blinded by the bubbles, slid and crashed into one another.

Tierney and Hellard, who trailed a block behind the rest, stopped their motorcycles and watched in horror. They silently agreed upon a plan of action: they spun their bikes around and fled from the scene.

The helicopter units, who watched the proceedings in utter amazement, were also inundated with the bubbles, which rose high and wide, blocking the view below.

"We're turning back! I repeat, we're turning back!" reported a pilot, and both choppers booked a hasty retreat.

Jamie and Darren cheered, and Lindsay smiled as they sped away.

IN A SMALL, dingy coffee shop fifty miles away, Darren and Jamie gave Lindsay the full details of their story. She, in turn, told them about the bottle and her talking dog, which helped Darren and Jamie figure out why the man in the restaurant had no idea who they were.

"Poor bum," said Darren. "The genie just took over his body for a moment."

"Cool!" said Jamie. "It's the *real* Invasion of the Body Snatchers!"

"Body *borrowers,* maybe," replied Darren. "This guy gives 'em back." Then, to Lindsay: "But why did you become an Arabian princess?"

"I always loved seeing movies about them when I was a kid," she explained. "Wouldn't you become one if you had the chance? I mean princes or kings?"

"Yeah, you know, uh, who wouldn't want a thing like that?" offered Darren. "But what made you decide to give it all up and come after us?"

"Well, I could say that I just wanted to help you guys, but really . . . I gave my cell phone to one of the servants, and he showed it to the king. He denounced me as a witch and sentenced me to hang by my arms in a dungeon till I croaked."

Jamie's eyes widened. "Rude!" he huffed.

"But weren't you, like, his daughter?" asked Darren.

"Yeah," she sighed, "but we'd grown apart during my late teens."

The boys exchanged a confused glance. "Well, never mind

that," said Darren, giving his head a shake. "Where is the bottle now?"

"Still in my kitchen, under the sink. I just used up my last wish on the bubble thing, though. Hey, do you think he'd give me more wishes if I rubbed the bottle again?"

"Probably not," said Darren, "but *I* haven't rubbed any bottle yet."

The three looked at each other.

"Well, what are we waiting for?" piped Lindsay. They plopped down money for the check and hurried out.

At the table behind theirs, a man whose face was buried in a menu turned and watched them go. His facial scar revealed his identity: Lance Wilson. He punched a number into his cell phone. A male voice answered with a "Yeah." It was Pauly, his Asian accomplice.

"The girl's apartment, under the sink," said Wilson. "Move now."

"Got it," said Pauly.

Wilson clicked out and punched in another number. "Hello, police?" he said. "I happen to know the whereabouts of a few kids you might be looking for."

Ozlo's bodyguard had been trailing the boys for weeks. His work finally paid off, and Ozlo's new plan had swung into action.

CHAPTER 17

The Ambush

AN UNEASY SILENCE prevailed in the private White House dining room. Two Secret Service men stood at attention while the nerve-racked First Lady sat at a formally adorned table, watching the father of her child stick his nose into a dish of nuts and seeds. Margaret Brady had begrudgingly accepted the fact that her husband was, at least for now, a guinea pig, and as absurd as it was (and as disgusting as the rodent seemed to her), she was doing her part to keep him sane. Not that she had to enjoy it. . . .

"Don't paw your food, just eat it," she snipped. The animal seemed to comply, taking a nibble. Its rapid teeth movements made Margaret wince. "Uchh," she muttered. She sensed a smile coming from one of the Secret Service men. "Oh, you think this is funny, do you?" she lobbed at him.

"No, ma'am," replied the man, lowering his head.

"That's good. Because if you laugh, you're fired."

The man hardened his face. The guinea pig stepped on

the seeds, causing them to scatter.

"Oh, that's just fine," scolded the First Lady. "Do you want your food or not?"

The second Secret Service man emitted a quiet whimper of a laugh. Margaret shot him a look, and he coughed, covering. She glared at him.

"Sorry, ma'am," he said, hoping that would end the matter.

He was saved by a knock on the door. Two aides entered.

"What?" the First Lady said sharply.

"Mrs. Brady, Mr. Spivack wants to inform you that the press conference is starting in a few minutes."

"So what? I'm not doing any press conference, and I'm certainly not going to sit and watch one."

"Umm . . . it's not you he wants."

Margaret looked at the animal, then at the aide. "You've got to be kidding!"

AT THE SAME MOMENT, the Fury III sped toward Lindsay's apartment. Darren was excited about the prospect of having his own three wishes.

"First, I'll turn the guinea pig back into the President, then I'll make us magicians again! We'll be bigger and better than before!"

"All right!" exclaimed Jamie. "What'll your *last* wish be?"

"I don't know. I'll save that one for a rainy day. Or maybe I'll save that one to *make* a rainy day. Haaa!" he chortled.

The car disappeared into a traffic tunnel between two buildings. Though it was dark, Lindsay instantly had a bad feeling. Her fears increased when the cars in front of her slowed to a crawl. The boys cursed the heavy traffic, but as light drew in from the end of the tunnel, they realized the problem: they were completely surrounded by a battalion of police vehicles. The trio had been soundly ambushed.

As they exited the tunnel, they looked around and realized they were stuck.

"Any ideas . . . anyone?" uttered Jamie.

"Fresh out," said Lindsay. "Darren?"

"Nothing here," he said sadly.

"Looks like we're stopping," said Lindsay.

The police led Lindsay's car to an empty lot at the side of the road and grinded to a halt. The police jumped out and surrounded the three, shielding themselves behind their vehicles. Tens of guns cocked at once.

Chief Belson spoke through a megaphone. "Come out slowly and keep your hands where we can see them. You're surrounded by sixty-eight police officers who don't like you."

Jamie started whimpering. "Don't cry," said Darren quietly, opening his door. "We just gotta be cool." Jamie struggled to comply, drying his tears as the three climbed out. Hambone peered out the back window.

"Turn around and place your hands on the car!" commanded Belson. It was Darren's turn to burst into tears as he complied with the command. Jamie joined in, weeping along side him.

"It's been fun, buddy," snorted Darren.

"We're too young to die," cried Jamie.

"Ucch, the two of you," scorned Lindsay. "Man up, huh? Get a grip." Embarrassed by the barb, they stopped crying.

A gleaming black limousine, escorted by four black Lincoln Town Cars, pulled up, and the officers cleared a path for them. A uniformed driver got out and opened the back door of the limo—Security Chief Tyler, Agent Stonewell, and three aides emerged. Assorted FBI men climbed out of the other vehicles.

Belson waved a hand and the police lowered their guns.

"We got 'em for you, Mr. Tyler," Belson said proudly.

"Good job, Chief," said Tyler.

"Thank you, sir."

Belson turned to direct some of his men, and Tyler noticed the Barney patch on his back. When Belson turned back to him, Tyler opened his mouth to comment, but realized he had no idea what to say. "Well, okay then," he muttered, and he approached the boys and Lindsay. "Hello, again."

"Hi," they said cautiously.

"You've pulled some very creative getaways, but I'm afraid that's all over now. You've got something we want. I think you know what it is, and I think you know *where* it is."

"Yes, we do," said Darren as the others nodded.

"It's in my apartment," said Lindsay plainly. There was no use trying to hide it now.

"Good. I'm glad you want to cooperate. That's very smart.

Well, let's not waste any more time. I believe there's enough security here to ensure us a relatively safe escort."

The officers chuckled as Tyler, Stonewell, and the others returned to the limo. Darren, Jamie, and Lindsay were led to one of the cars behind it. The driver opened the back door and an officer handed Lindsay her dog.

"Hambone!" she chirped, and the three climbed into the vehicle.

The police and government motorcade took over the town, storming through the busy city streets, sirens wailing.

"They seem to know where I live," said Lindsay as they neared her building.

"That's not a tough one," said Darren, "but how did they know we had the bottle?" His friends' blank faces revealed their common cluelessness.

"What'll happen when they get it?" Jamie wondered aloud.

"They'll have the genie and then . . . they won't need us anymore," surmised Darren. "Nor will they want anyone besides them knowing what they know." They shuddered at the thought. "Listen, Lindsay, I'm sorry we got you involved at all. You can get out of this anytime, though. It's us they want."

"With me knowing everything?" said Lindsay. "I don't think so. Anyway, I don't mind being in this with you guys. She turned to Jamie. "You're really funny," she said, and, to Darren, "and you're kind of cute. You know, for a fifteen-year-old."

"Ha-haaaaaa!" chortled Jamie, pointing a finger at Darren. "She thinks you're cute!"

"I heard the girl. Stop pointing at me!" Darren shoved Jamie's hand away. He paused, not knowing how to reply. "I think you're . . . really nice," he tried.

"Thanks," she said.

"And pretty, too," he added, unable to look at her. *Really pretty.*

"Thanks twice," she said.

"And, uh . . . ummm . . ."

"Don't blow it, that was good," she said.

"Okay," said Darren, relieved.

IN THE WHITE HOUSE Press Room, Arnold Spivack—the forty-five-year-old, brown-haired, baby-faced Press Secretary—bravely faced a mob of reporters who were alarmed by President Brady's continually cancelled appearances. The strange presence of a caged guinea pig on a table next to Spivack's podium had so far been ignored. Spivack was following Agent Stonewell's advice to the letter, which meant the President's attendance at the conference was mandatory no matter how strange it seemed.

"Sir, the question is very simple," said a frustrated news correspondent. "Where is the President? Has anyone besides you seen him in the last two days?"

"Of course they have," said Spivack. "He just has some top-secret business that is taking all of his time, and he will be back before you all very shortly."

"What is the nature of this top-secret business?" continued the correspondent. "I think the public has a right to know." Others in the room strongly voiced their agreement.

"When the time is right, you'll all be informed," replied Spivack. "Until then, the best I can do is again offer my apologies from the President himself. You have my personal assurance that, uh, nothing is the matter."

"Why is that hamster up there?" a reporter called out.

"He's a guinea pig," corrected Spivack. "And, uh, I just thought you all might want to give the new White House pet a warm Washington welcome." Spivack turned to the animal and clapped loudly, fully expecting the assemblage to join in. They didn't. After a short, embarrassing silence, a reporter raised a hand. "Yes," said Spivack, clearing his throat and struggling to retain his dignity.

"What's the animal's name?"

"His name? Why, uh, we like to call him Mr. President," he said, adding a nervous chuckle.

"Oh, then maybe *he'd* like to answer a few questions for us," chided another reporter, causing a few snickers.

"Yeah, why no word on the new tax bill, Mr. President?" ribbed another. "Does Congress have you caged in?"

The room broke out in laughter as Spivack's nerves neared their breaking point. The guinea pig seemed agitated, manically climbing and gnawing the bars.

"Look, he's *still* trying to get out of it!" said the reporter, to the further amusement of the room. Spivack, sensing the

President's discomfort, stepped in front of the cage.

"Okay, that will be all, ladies and gentlemen. Thank you very much."

The cage was quickly whisked away as the reporters murmured their displeasure. One of them answered his cell phone and took down information. He turned to a colleague.

"That was MacEwen. There's something going on at the Lincoln Memorial."

"What?"

"Not sure exactly. Something about a magician, and it may relate to the President somehow."

"Then let's get there before all these chowderheads do," said the colleague, and they scurried out.

The sounds of ringing cell phones suddenly filled the room. Everyone answered, scribbled down info, and hurriedly set out to the Lincoln Memorial.

WHEN THE MOTORCADE arrived at Lindsay's building, Tyler released Chief Belson and his army of officers with a simple, "Thanks, we'll take it from here." He didn't want them knowing any more than they needed to.

The rest followed Lindsay up to her apartment. Darren and Jamie, Security Chief Tyler, Agent Stonewell, two aides, and four FBI men crowded in behind her as she entered.

"Welcome to my little home," said Lindsay. "Can I get anyone anything? Soda? Cookies? A chance to rule the universe?"

"The bottle, please, thank you," said Stonewell, chomping at the bit to hold the supernatural wonder in her hands. It was to be the greatest moment of her life; the crowning achievement of her career.

"Okay, then. One genie bottle coming right up," said Lindsay. She reached into the cabinet below the sink and pulled out . . . a glass flower vase. "Oh, wait, hold on." She looked in and pulled out brushes, cleansers, and sponges. "I left it here, I swear."

"We don't have all day," said Tyler. "Just give us the bottle and you're free to go."

Darren and Jamie exchanged hopeful glances, then peered at the FBI men. Their stern faces did little to quell their fears.

Lindsay cleared out the entire cabinet and came up empty. "I don't understand this!" she said. "I put it right here before I went to Arabia!"

"Arabia?" said Stonewell.

"Oh, yeah, it was my first wish. I was an Arabian princess. I could have become queen someday if the king didn't want to strap me up on a meat hook."

"Young lady, this is a very urgent matter," said Tyler. "I suggest you find the bottle right now before—" His cell phone rang, and he grabbed it from his pocket. "Yeah? . . . I see. . . . Yes, yes. . . . Will do. Okay." He turned to Lindsay. "Turn on channel seven."

Lindsay picked up the TV remote and clicked her set on. A news show aired a live segment from the steps of the Lincoln

Memorial. The white marble building stood solid, its forty-four-foot columns framing the enormous statue of Abraham Lincoln. Standing atop its immense staircase was a confident, charismatic Amazing Ozlo, who was being interviewed by a famous black newswoman named Kim Granger.

"It's Ozlo!" said Jamie.

On TV, sightseers gathered around, goaded on by Lance Wilson, who announced through a megaphone, "Step right up, ladies and gentlemen, boys and girls! The Amazing Ozlo is about to perform!" The intimidating Pauly stood off to the side, arms folded. It was growing dark, and powerful searchlights surged on, illuminating the premises.

"Tell me, Ozlo," said the newswoman. "Why are you doing this show unrehearsed and, apparently, at the spur of the moment?"

"Because, Kim, I was so proud of my newest act that I wanted the world to see it as soon as possible. I've invented wonders that scientists and philosophers have never even dreamed of. Wonders that exceed the most fertile imagination."

"Does this have anything to do with the fact that the newest magic sensation, Jackson and Jenks, have surpassed you in popularity, even replacing you as White House entertainer?"

Ozlo produced a fake laugh. "Oh, Kim, people always like to embrace whatever's the latest thing, but after today, I'm afraid those two will be forgotten, and *my* name will be back on the lips of the public. The world will know who's *really* the greatest magician who ever lived. I give you my personal guarantee of that."

"Wow, okay, I hope you're right. Can you tell us what you're going to do?"

"I'd rather surprise you, really, but I can tell you that President Brady himself will be here . . . in one form or another."

"Well, then you're the only one outside the White House who seems to know where he is, Ozlo. I wish you the best of luck."

"Thanks, Kim."

"He's got the bottle," said Darren, his eyes transfixed to the screen.

"He's right," said Stonewell. "Let's go."

CHAPTER 18

The Greatest
Show on Earth

DARREN, JAMIE, AND LINDSAY sat across from Tyler and
the others in the limo. Their fear of losing their lives was now
replaced with the fear of what the crazed Ozlo might do with
the greatest power in the world. *It couldn't be any worse than
what the government wants to do with it,* thought Darren.

"Can this thing move any faster?" Tyler barked.

"I'm doing the best I can, sir," replied the driver.

They watched the show unfold on the limo's TV screen.
The now-teeming crowd gazed up at Ozlo, who stood at the
center of the Lincoln Memorial. He said, "Flags, appear!" and
two glorious twenty-foot high United States flags popped out
from his hands. He waved them about, shouting, "Let's strike
up the band!" A wide billow of smoke blew from the ground,
and a twenty-piece brass band magically appeared behind him,
playing "Stars and Stripes Forever." The crowd went crazy,

marveling at the patriotic, eye-popping display.

"How on earth did *he* get the bottle?" said Tyler. The question went unanswered.

Scores of TV cameras, perched atop news vans, were trained on Ozlo as he finished his opening effect: Two pretty female assistants waved the flags in front of Ozlo's hands. When they yanked them away, Ozlo was holding a Bald Eagle on his outstretched arm. The crowd cheered as the magnificent bird flapped its wings. A puff of smoke, and a second Bald Eagle appeared on his other arm. Ozlo released both animals—they flew over the audience and up, up, and away.

"Let freedom ring!" exclaimed Ozlo to an avalanche of applause.

Other news vans pulled up around the site. Cameramen and reporters spilled out, scrambling to get the show on the air.

In the government limo, the six discussed their options. "We'll have him taken by force," said Tyler.

"No!" said Darren. "You have no idea what he could do to anyone who comes near him."

"What could he do?" asked Tyler.

"Anything," replied Stonewell.

"What do you mean? How could he possibly—"

"May I remind you of the President's current state?" said Stonewell. "The wish-bearer can do anything imaginable. He can dispose of anyone he wants. This will have to be a covert operation, so I suggest we don't show up in a stretch limousine."

Tyler weighed the information. "Driver, take us down Twenty-third. We'll park behind the memorial."

"LADIES AND GENTLEMEN," Ozlo boomed over the sound system. "You are about to see sights that will astound and amaze! First, a few little numbers I dreamed up just last night. Watch!"

A female assistant stepped inside a tall, open box, on top of which was a huge spiral blade. Ozlo closed the front of the box and switched on a motor. The blade spun with a violent roar and sank into the box, creating the illusion that the woman was most certainly being sliced and diced.

"It's the Amazing Ozlo's new diet dream!" he said over the sound of whirring and grinding. "It gives every woman the chance to instantly become . . . slinky!"

He opened the front of the box. The woman seemed unharmed, but there was something odd about her, almost macabre—there appeared to be thin diagonal lines across her face and body. Then, eerily, the top of the woman's head fell forward, and the audience gasped—she'd been sliced into a giant human Slinky. Her upper torso cascaded forward in a perfect arc, her skin fanning out like an accordion, and the rest of her body followed behind. Her head hit the ground, and her torso and legs lifted and flipped up and over the top of her. Her feet hit the first step, and, just like the famous toy, her body sprung up and over them. The Slinky effect continued with her legs flipping over onto a lower step. The audience was astonished, though many grimaced, creeped out by the bizarre effect.

The human Slinky finally hit the bottom of the platform and came to rest on her feet. Two male assistants tried to carry her back up, but ran into trouble—one grabbed her head, and the other, her legs, but the spring affect caused her middle to clunk to the ground. The audience laughed as the men hauled her up the stairs, her torso springing about behind her.

"Okay, that is *so* gross," mumbled a gum-chewing teenage girl in the crowd.

The assistants stood the Slinky woman up, Ozlo waved his hand, and she instantly returned her to her original, healthy state. She smiled and waved to the audience, who whooped and applauded.

"There's lots more to go," bellowed Ozlo, "but these great stone columns are blocking your view. Well, that's no problem for me. Watch! Columns, move now!"

He clapped his hands, and the four centermost columns guarding the front of the memorial emitted a booming rumble. The pillars, as if motorized, neatly snapped away from the roof and lowered themselves into the platform until their tops were flush with the floor. The audience shouted in disbelief and applauded resoundingly. The Amazing Ozlo could indeed do anything.

"Now, how would you like to see one of the great American presidents come to life?" bellowed Ozlo. The audience roared its approval. "He freed the slaves, but can he free himself?

Ladies and gentlemen, I give you the sixteenth president of the United States—Abraham Lincoln!"

Instantly, a low vibration emanated from the center of the building. Ozlo stepped aside and the impossible occurred.

The statue of Lincoln began to move.

The audience gasped and lurched back in shock as the one hundred and twenty ton stone likeness issued thunderous cracking sounds. It slowly budged a hand, an arm, its head, and then, as if busting from steel restraints, it lifted itself up and out of its permanent chair. Heavy blocks of loose rock plunged to the ground around it, shattering into pieces. The tall, square block it stood upon slowly sank, breaking into the platform below it until the statue's feet were resting on the floor.

Some audience members screamed, overwhelmed by the sight. The gum-chewing teenage girl stood frozen, her jaw hanging open. The gum fell from her mouth.

Reporter Kim Granger, grasping her microphone, could only utter, "Oh . . . my . . . God." Virtually all of the reporters were, for the first time ever, collectively speechless.

"This ought to give 'em a thrill," Ozlo whispered to Wilson.

He was right. Viewers across the country and around the globe were frantically phoning one another, spouting in their respective languages, "Turn on the news right now! You're not going to believe this!"

The white marble President Lincoln seemed to observe

the throng of faces below him, then took a step forward. The ground shook with the weight of each five-ton shoe. The crowd, enthralled but uneasy, remained motionless. The stone giant took another step, then another. He stood at the foot of the staircase and turned his head, taking in the entire court. When he painstakingly opened his mouth to speak, his deep voice reverberated for miles.

"Four score and seven years ago," he bellowed, "our fathers brought forth on this continent a new nation, conceived in liberty, and dedicated to the proposition that all men are created equal." He stretched out his arms. "God Bless America!"

The band struck up "Hail to the Chief" as the crowd erupted, clapping, whistling, and cheering.

Lincoln turned and lumbered back to his chair. Ozlo said the word, and the block platform rose. All the loose pieces flew back into place and it was again an inert, solid statue.

"My God," Kim Granger gushed into her news camera. "I have never seen anything like this! It's as if miracles are occurring! The Amazing Ozlo is back and he's taking no prisoners. One can only imagine what Jackson and Jenks would have to do to top this unbelievable display of absolute genius!"

Darren, Jamie, Lindsay, and the White House crew reached the side of the structure. They hid behind a row of hedges and whispered as Ozlo took a bow.

"What do we do now?" said Tyler.

"There it is!" said Lindsay, watching the stage.

"What?" said Stonewell.

"That's the bottle!" She pointed to the genie bottle on a

table with other magic equipment, just behind the band.

"Let's grab it," said Tyler.

"No, no," said Darren. "The genie is under his control now, no matter what. It only gives its powers to one person at a time."

"He's right," confirmed Stonewell. "It's useless to us right now."

"There must be something we can do," said Tyler.

Darren thought hard. "Jamie, there was something the genie said in the thrift shop. The wishing powers could be transferred to someone else somehow."

"Yeah, right," said Jamie, straining to recall the conversation. "No, wait. It's only if the guy who's got the wishes says for it to happen . . . out loud."

"Bummer," said Stonewell dryly.

Ozlo was ready for his finale—the trick that would insure him a place in the history books. "Ladies and gentleman, I have just one more illusion to perform. For it, I need a guinea pig. And I mean a *real* guinea pig. One from, let's say, the White House!"

AT THAT MOMENT, in the White House, two male aides returned the caged guinea pig to the Oval Office. Talking among themselves, they missed the sight of the guinea pig disappearing into thin air. They finally looked at the cage.

"Where is he?"

"He's gone!"

A PUFF OF SMOKE arose on the platform of the Lincoln Memorial, and the guinea pig appeared on a table next to Ozlo. There was a smattering of applause as Ozlo smiled and picked up the animal.

"Ladies and gentlemen, I give you a very special guinea pig indeed. This little rodent, believe it or not, is none other than the President of the United States!" The crowd chuckled. "In a moment, I will prove to you that I am perfectly serious. But first, I don't think the role of guinea pig befits a man of the President's stature, so let's make him into something a bit taller. How about . . . a *giraffe?*"

The guinea pig's shape rapidly changed. Its head shot up toward the roof of the structure, lifted by the sudden appearance of a long, thick neck. Its body expanded like a balloon, while its gray fur turned a spotted orange, yellow, and brown. Its torso jettisoned upward as lengthy legs formed beneath it.

Everyone watched in open-mouthed amazement, with the possible exception of Darren, who shook his head. "I could have gone all day without seeing a lousy giraffe," he muttered as the audience went wild.

Stonewell was nervous. "The President can't take this and come out sane if he comes out at all! We have to act now!"

"What are we going to do?" asked Tyler.

"Let me go up and talk to him," said Jamie. "He likes me."

"What? No!" yelled Darren, but Jamie leaped onto the platform.

"Ozlo!" he called out. "Hey, Ozlo!"

Ozlo turned and was very surprised to see the boy he considered to be his greatest enemy. "Well, well, well, look who's here, ladies and gentlemen! It's Jamie the Magnificent!"

The audience applauded as Jamie amiably walked toward him. "Listen, dude," he said, "you've got to stop what you're doing. The President might not be able to take it!"

"Did you hear that, ladies and gentlemen? The great Jamie Jenks says I should stop what I'm doing. Do *you* think I should stop what I'm doing?"

The audience voiced a resounding "No!" and booed Jamie.

"Do you think he's jealous?" continued Ozlo. "Maybe he and his little friend could never do anything quite as great as I can!"

"No, Ozlo, I'm serious!" said Jamie. "That's the real President, and he might go insane if you keep doing this!"

"He says the President might go insane, ladies and gentlemen. Don't you think that idea's a little, uh . . . insane?" The audience chuckled. "You're interrupting my show, young man, but I think I can use you. The giraffe looks hungry, and he only eats . . . plants!" Ozlo muttered under his breath, and instantly, leaves sprouted from Jamie's thin body. Within seconds, he completely morphed into a potted ficus plant.

"Jamie!" yelled Darren as the audience applauded, certain this was part of the act.

"God in heaven," Stonewell whispered. Lindsay and Tyler

stood stunned, as did the aides and the FBI men.

"Let's see if the giraffe wants to eat half of a magic duo!" said Ozlo. The assistants turned the giraffe around to face the green, inert Jamie.

"Stooooooooooooooop!" screamed Darren, sprinting onto the stage.

"Darren!" shouted Lindsay, but her fearful cry went unheard. Darren ran in front of the giraffe, blocking it from the plant.

"Oh, look, it's the other half of the team," said Ozlo. "It's Darren Jackson, ladies and gentlemen!"

The audience applauded Darren's appearance, anticipating more fantastic illusions. Instead, Darren gritted his teeth and delivered a roundhouse punch—he hit Ozlo squarely on the jaw and knocked him to the ground. The crowd gasped as Wilson and Pauly ran up and attacked Darren, locking his arms behind him. Two female assistants tried to help Ozlo, but he brusquely waved them off and gave his head a shake. He propped himself up on one arm, wiping a trickle of blood from his lips.

"Don't even think about it, Ozlo!" yelled Darren. "Turn him back right now!"

"Now, that is what I call professional jealousy, ladies and gentlemen," yelled Ozlo. "Are you going to stand for that?" The audience booed Darren. "Well, neither am I!" A look of fright crossed Darren's face as Ozlo pointed a finger at him.

Another voice rang out. "Stop right there!"

That came from Ainsley Grosspucker. Ozlo spun around and was visibly thrown by the surprise appearance.

"Ainsley, no! *Run!*" yelled Darren, struggling to free himself from Wilson and Pauly's vice-like grips. Ainsley stayed his ground.

"Well, look who showed up," said Ozlo, regaining his composure. "I never thought I'd see your ugly mug again. Ladies and gentlemen, this is indeed a day of surprises! It's my own baby brother, Ainsley! How about a hand for 'Little Ainsley?'" The crowd applauded politely.

Darren looked over to Lindsay, who was scared and teary. "*His brother?*" mouthed Darren.

"Don't hurt them! I'm warning you!" threatened Ainsley.

"Oh, what are you going to do to me, Ainsley? Book me for a birthday party? Cheat me out of money like you do all of your acts? I don't think so, you little weasel!"

The audience, sensing Ozlo was serious, murmured uncomfortably.

"Jamie and Darren are good people and they don't deserve this!" cried Ainsley.

"This is none of your business!" shouted Ozlo.

"Yes, it is! They're my clients and my friends! What would Mother say if she saw what you were doing?"

This had the unfortunate effect of triggering the innermost reserves of Ozlo's rage. "*Who cares about Mother?*" he thundered. "She didn't love me! She *never* loved me! She only loved *you,* and that was because you groveled at her feet!"

"How can you even *think* that, Fernadel!" said Ainsley.

"Fernadel?" the audience murmured. Darren, meanwhile, racked his brain to figure a way out of this.

"I told you never to call me that!" exploded Ozlo. "You are a bad, bad man, Ainsley! That's why you are going to spend the rest of your life as the weasel that you are! *Make him a weasel!"*

Without a beat, Ainsley's body imploded, shrinking furiously, until he became a small white weasel. He flitted about the platform, searching for a hole to escape to.

The audience gasped, and, deciding that it *was* part of the act after all, they laughed and applauded anew. The giraffe, meanwhile, turned its attention to Jamie, the ficus tree. Darren grunted, still trying futilely to wriggle free from the bodyguards' grips.

Lindsay, off to the side, put her shaking hands to her mouth, expecting the worst.

"And you!" said Ozlo, swinging back to Darren. "You are the reason why all this has to happen. You tried to outdo me. Well, you can't outdo me! No one will ever outdo me! *I am the greatest magician ever!"* He raised his hands dramatically, ready to dispose of his foe.

Darren had an idea—a final, desperate attempt. He yelled, "No, you're not, Ozlo! We're greater magicians than you can ever *hope* to be!"

Ozlo responded with a phrase that Darren heard him say a few times before—

"Yeah, *you wish!*"

Ozlo instantly felt a power-surge rage through his body, and he grimaced in shock. A green and blue laser-bright light enveloped Ozlo, then shot out of him. It disappeared into Darren with an ear-splitting scream. Terrified, Wilson and Pauly released Darren and ran for cover.

"What's happening?" shouted Howard Tyler.

"A transfer of control, I think!" said Stonewell. "Ozlo sent the force's powers into Darren!"

"That's good, isn't it?" asked the confused Security Chief.

"Yes, that's good!"

Stonewell was correct. Ozlo realized with horror that the magic had left him completely.

Darren smiled and said, "Mirror, mirror on the wall, who's the greatest magician of all? I wish for that to be me!" He braced himself for the inevitable rush of wind that struck immediately from behind the crowd, taking all by surprise. TV reporters dropped microphones, news writers' notebooks went flying, and cameramen struggled with their equipment. The wind hit the stage, wreaking havoc, and, just as before, it quickly stopped cold.

The jarred audience struggled to regain their footing while Darren wasted no time in tackling his first order of business. "Plant, turn back into Jamie!" The plant promptly transformed into his friend, who took a moment to realize that his body had returned.

"Awesome!" said Jamie.

"I won't forget this, Jackson!" threatened Ozlo.

"Good, let's make sure of that. You know who never forgets? Elephants! You're an elephant!" And there it was—Ozlo's face and body pushed, pulled, and grew until the audience saw before them a howling, stomping, gray pachyderm. They gasped and applauded yet again.

"Stay right there, elephant!" commanded Darren, and Ozlo was unable to move his back legs. The giraffe, however, had no such restraints. Startled by the elephant's appearance, it bolted down the steps. The audience panicked and shoved one another, fleeing the runaway animal. A few fell into the reflecting pool behind them.

"Giraffe, stop!" yelled Darren. "Turn into the President!"

The audience turned back in time to see the giraffe's neck and body shrinking. Within seconds, President Brady was standing on the steps, his suit and tie a rumpled mess. The crowd erupted with joyous cheering and shouting, and the band reprised "Hail to the Chief." The President looked around, bewildered at first, then happy as he realized he was quite himself once again. He waved and smiled, accepting the accolades.

Lindsay, Stonewell, Tyler, and the aides were beaming and applauding.

"He's back, Mr. Vice President," said Tyler on his cell phone, practically in tears. "The President is back. . . . What, Sir? . . . Yes, the bottle. It's in our sight and we'll get it right now." He clicked off the phone and turned to the aides. "Go!"

The aides sprinted up the steps.

"No! Stop!" hollered Stonewell. "You could ruin every-thing!"

But the aides raced to the bottle. Competing to grab it, however, they knocked the table over. The bottle flew off and rolled up behind Darren, darting through his legs. Darren leaped toward it, but was practically tackled by the aides, who continued after it.

The bottle headed toward Ozlo the elephant. The giant mammal, seemingly aware of the situation, bucked up on his anchored hind legs and tried to grab it. Unfortunately, Ozlo's hands were now heavy round feet.

"NOOOOOOOOOOOOOOO!" shouted Darren, and *crush*—the elephant squashed the bottle, flattening it paper-thin.

Stonewell was crestfallen. "That's it."

"*What's it?*" asked Tyler.

"It's over, I think," said Stonewell. "No, I'm sure of it. The genie is released. It's freed."

"Is that good or bad?" yelled Tyler, exhausted from the excitement.

He would have his answer in a second. The assemblage onstage and off, and those watching on TV, witnessed a spectacular sight. Smoke and light billowed from the flattened bottle, whirling in circles on the platform with a haunting *whistle*. In the folds of the smoke, forms of people appeared and vanished. They were the virtual memories of the hundreds of identities the genie had momentarily stepped into over the centuries. Each was being released from the genie's data banks—the final step in the alien force's freedom. The apparitions came and went with increasing speed. Some were in togas, some in robes, some in seventeenth century finery. One was a surgeon, one an airline stewardess, and one was unquestionably an orangutan.

The speed of the ghostly appearances reached a fever pitch until each was no more than a blip. Their pace slowed as the cycle finished, ending with the man from the thrift shop, then Hambone, and lastly, Wilson, whose body the genie had used to grant wishes to Ozlo.

The spinning, billowing smoke then thrust itself five hundred feet in the air, and an explosion burst within its folds. It blasted outward, forming a sky-darkening cloud, with flashes of white light dancing within. Balls of light and smoke shot out from its center and flew back toward the Lincoln Memorial.

One bolt hit the elephant and another struck the weasel, which had found refuge in a patch of dirt. Instantaneously, both animals shifted back to their original human forms. Ozlo collapsed to the ground, exhausted. Ainsley found himself lying behind a bush, covered with dirt and stones. He wiped himself off while catching his breath.

The light and smoke balls then hit the band members who vanished in a shock of brightness. Another ball hit the tops of the four front pillars, which quickly boomed back up and locked into place.

A final ball hit Darren—he flew backward into a column, but made no physical change at all. He shook himself off and looked skyward, marveling at the whirling, smoking mass above him. Along with Jamie, President Brady, and the others, he shielded his eyes from the bright beams.

Suddenly, the gargantuan cloud soared higher and exploded once again, ballooning out in a burst of golden fireworks as wide as three football fields. The brilliant display lingered in the air, slowly and surely forming a circular pattern. The lines of the pattern materialized further, and everyone came to realize what they were seeing.

It was a flying saucer. A UFO.

It wasn't made of metal or glass, but of golden light, smoke, and mist. They could see through it, as if it were the ghost of a ship rather than a solid object. It came clearly into focus, and tens of thousands of brightly colored lights appeared all around it. Several separate layers formed above its base, each growing progressively narrower, and the outlines of windows could be seen around the hull. A huge flat disk at the top cast an eerie bluish glow over the mass.

No one moved or spoke as they stared up in awe. The ship suddenly blinded the onlookers with stark white lights and gusting winds as it began to revolve. It spun faster as it rose into the sky, then shot straight upward. And, with a final sonic *boom,* it disappeared entirely. The roar lingered for twenty seconds, and silence and smoke was all that remained.

For a moment, everyone stood shocked and numb, overwhelmed by the experience. They all turned toward President

Brady, who remained frozen on the top step, unsure of what to do. Darren, thinking fast, ran to the President, grabbed his hand, and lifted it victoriously.

"And that's our show!" yelled Darren.

The crowd went crazy, shouting and cheering. Lindsay jumped up and down, gleefully squealing. Ozlo, no longer an elephant, now bore the look of a stunned cow.

Tyler wiped sweat from his face and turned to Agent Stonewell. "Does this mean Jackson is the only one with magic powers?"

"No," replied Stonewell. "I think he'll find that he's just normal again. The genie and his powers are gone. Forever."

Though maybe not, thought Stonewell. There was one detail about the whole affair that she'd kept completely private. There was, according to the scrolls, a second bottle. Someday, she vowed, she'd find it . . . herself.

Every newsperson gleefully aired live reports. Kim Granger was beside herself with exuberance: "You saw it here live, ladies and gentlemen—the most spectacular display of magic, illusion, and Hollywood lighting effects ever witnessed, presented jointly by The Amazing Ozlo and Jackson and Jenks! *Mind-blowing* is all this reporter can say! If you didn't know better, you would almost think it was real!"

The crowd dispersed, talking animatedly as Secret Service men rushed the stage. They whisked the President away and handcuffed Ozlo.

"What? What is this?" protested Ozlo.

"You're under arrest," said a Secret Service man.

"For what?"

"Kidnapping the President. That's a federal offense."

"He was a guinea pig!"

"Tell it to the judge, pal," said the man, dragging him off.

"Later, Ozlo!" Jamie called after him. "Great working with you!"

"What?" piped Darren. "Why are you being nice to him? That freak almost killed you!"

"Nah, he just turned me into a plant. The *giraffe* almost killed me."

"Man, you are something else."

"Hey, guys," said Lindsay, approaching them. "That wasn't a bad show," she said with a smirk.

"Thanks," chuckled Darren. "We had a little help, but it was all my idea." Lindsay giggled.

"Hey, *you're* the magician now, dude!" exclaimed Jamie.

"Not anymore, man," said Darren. "My magic powers are history. The genie escaped and took them all with him."

"No more wishes?" asked Lindsay.

"Gone for good," confirmed Darren, "and you know what? Thank God for that. Nothing but trouble, all that fame and power. From now on, I'm just plain Darren. Nothing more, nothing less, and that is just fine with me."

"Does this mean we have to go back to working and studying for school?" asked Jamie.

"Yep," said Darren. "And frankly, I can't wait. Of course, we still have the mansion, though."

"Partayyyyy!" yelled Jamie. The boys laughed and high-fived each other.

Ainsley approached them. "Hey, guys."

"Ainsley!" yelled the boys, patting him on the back.

"Hey, thanks for trying to save us, Ainsley," said Darren.

"Yeah, you really did us a solid, man," added Jamie.

"Oh, it was nothing, really," said Ainsley.

"You never told us that Ozlo, or, uh, *Fernadel* was your brother," said Darren.

"I've always tried to ignore that fact," said Ainsley. "We hadn't spoken since he ran off with my wife."

"He stole your wife?" said Darren.

"Yeah, Nadine."

"Nadine, the *supermodel?*" asked Jamie.

"That's the one. I thought she'd be good in his act—*he* thought she'd be good, well, elsewhere, too. They left me high and dry. I was thinking of ending it all before I met you guys."

"Well, I'm glad you didn't, because it worked out well for all of us," said Darren. "We're not magicians anymore, though. That's all over."

"I thought that might be the case," said Ainsely plainly.

"But, hey," continued Darren, "at least you have your commission, and we have our house and all the money you're keeping for us."

"Uh, guys, we need to talk about that."

"What about it?" said Darren.

"I haven't always been the best businessman. The house isn't actually, uh, paid for—at all—and I lost all the money gambling at the track."

"*You lost our money gambling on horses?*" piped Darren.

"Well, not all of it. See, my brother was right. I *was* a weasel. The contract I had you sign actually called for *you* to get ten percent and for *me* to get ninety. Just my own little weasely trick. But now, here—I want you to have everything that's left from our account." He handed Darren a check. Jamie peered over his shoulder.

"Four hundred dollars and twenty-eight cents?" said Darren.

"I know it's not a lot, but it's all we have. I'm really sorry. I'll try to make it up to you in any way I can."

Darren groaned and threw up his hands in frustration.

"Now, I'll see you guys later," continued Ainsley. "I got a call from the coast. I'm moving to LA to join a big talent agency, thanks to you!"

"Hey, that's great!" said Jamie.

"Oh, yeah . . . *wonderful,*" said Darren, disgusted.

Ainsley took off down the stairs. "I'll call you!" he said. "I promise I'll help you as soon as I can!"

"Great! Bye, Ainsley!" said Jamie. "And thanks!"

"Later," Darren managed. Ainsley was gone.

"He's going to help us!" said Jamie. "We'll get to buy another house!"

"Man, if he helps us, I'll *eat* a house. That dude's a goner."

"Yeah? Hey, what about Inga? Maybe she'll stick around."

"Sure, she'll move right in with you and your mother. Forget about it, Jamie. Ah, this turned out awful. A total bust."

Jamie then noticed four men walking toward them. Two were the aides Jamie saw in the White House men's room. Trailing them were the two scary-looking men in black turtlenecks.

"Darren!" said Jamie, trembling.

"What?"

"It's them! The guys from the bathroom!"

"The bathroom?"

"You know, in the White House! Those are the guys who said—"

"Hello, Jamie and Darren," said an aide amiably. "How are you doing?"

"Uh, fine," replied Jamie nervously.

"My name is Roger Collins. I'm the new head of White House Special Services."

"Hello," said Darren.

"I just want to let you know that the President will be sending you both special commendations for your part in saving his life. We're not certain how it all happened to begin with, but, well, we'll just keep that to ourselves, huh?" Everyone chuckled. "So, on behalf of the United States government, I thank you for your service to our country."

"Thank *you*," offered the boys, plenty relieved.

"Oh, and one more thing." The boys froze in fear as the man reached inside his jacket and pulled out—an envelope, which he handed to Darren. "The Department of Defense would like to meet with you. They heard about a secret weapon you have in your house that laid waste to eight FBI agents. They want to buy the rights from you to possibly use as their own secret weapon."

"Oh, it's nothing like that," said Darren. "It was our dirt and garbage-busting Super—"

Jamie slapped a hand over Darren's mouth. "Super Weapon," he finished. "We'll be happy to meet with them as soon as possible."

"Good. Just call, and an assistant will take care of everything. Thank you again and good luck." They all shook hands, and Collins and the others left. Indeed, the newly reassigned men no longer posed any threat to the boys.

"Did you hear that?" exclaimed Darren. "They want to buy the Super Suckers!"

"The Super *Weapons,* okay?" said Jamie. "We'll let *them* be the suckers."

"Wow, who's the smart one now?" chuckled Lindsay. "Looks like the tables have turned, huh?"

"You know, she's right, Jamie," said Darren. "You're really pretty smart sometimes, pal. I mean, you know, in your own way."

"Thanks, Darren. Hey, do you think I'll be able to get another pony with the money we get from the government?"

"Another pony? What happened to the first one? I never saw any pony."

"Oh, he ran away. I forgot to get a barn." Darren and

Lindsay were speechless. "Kidding!" said Jamie. "Never got a pony!" The three broke out laughing, and Jamie and Lindsay began rehashing the events of the last hour together.

Darren, meanwhile, sighed deeply and looked around, thinking about all that had happened in the space of two and a half months. He'd been famous, he'd been rich, and he'd been, for a few short minutes, the most powerful man in the universe. But right now, he thought, he was just a bit hungry and also a little worried. How do you follow a summer like this one? Would there ever be anything greater for him to experience in life, even as young as he was? Would starting his junior year in school next week make him forget all the excitement? Would people forget that he and Jamie had been famous and just treat them like normal kids again? He sincerely hoped so. The thoughts made him feel tired, and a bit sad and empty.

Lindsay noticed Darren's pensive state. "A penny for your thoughts?"

"Oh, I was just thinking, you know . . . about how hungry I am right now."

"Good! Let's go eat," she said.

"Where we gonna go?" asked Jamie.

"You guys ever been to that place called Ali Baba's?" she asked. "I've always wanted to try it, and it's just a few blocks away from here."

Darren laughed. "Sure, whatever you want . . . Princess!"

"Let's go!" yelled Jamie. "Last one there's gotta pay!"

The three scampered down the stairs, laughing and yelling like children. Lindsay jumped up and ran along the edge of the reflecting pool. Darren grabbed her hand to steady her, and they ran along the pond, hand in hand.

The real magic, it seemed, was only just beginning.